THE IRON MAIN GATE OF JABBA'S PALACE SCRAPED OPEN HARSHLY, OILED ONLY WITH SAND AND TIME. STANDING OUTSIDE IN THE DUSTY GALE WAS LUKE SKYWALKER.

Resolutely, Luke strode

Almost immediately, tw... blocking his path. Luke raised his ... guards. Before they could draw weapons, they were clutching at their throats, choking, gasping.

Luke lowered his hand and walked on. The guards didn't follow.

As Luke entered Jabba's court, the level of tumult dropped.

Luke let Jabba fill his mind totally. 'You will bring Captain Solo and the Wookiee to me.'

Jabba smiled grimly. 'Your mind powers will not work on me, boy.'

Luke altered his stance somewhat. 'Nevertheless, I am taking Captain Solo and his friends. You can either profit from this . . . or be destroyed. But I warn you not to underestimate my powers.'

Jabba laughed the laugh of a lion cautioned by a mouse. 'There will be no bargain, young Jedi. I shall enjoy watching you die.'

The floor suddenly dropped away, sending Luke crashing into the pit below . . .

RETURN OF THE JEDI™

Starring

**Mark
Hamill**

**Harrison
Ford**

**Carrie
Fisher**

**Billy Dee
Williams**

**Anthony
Daniels**
as C-3PO

Directed by
Richard Marquand

Produced by
Howard Kazanjian

Screenplay by
**Lawrence Kasdan and
George Lucas**

Story by
George Lucas

Executive Producer
George Lucas

Music by
John Williams

A Lucasfilm Ltd. Production — A Twentieth Century-Fox Release

James Kahn

Return of the Jedi

Screenplay by Lawrence Kasdan and George Lucas
Story by George Lucas

Futura
Macdonald & Co
London & Sydney

A Futura Book

First full-length edition published in Great Britain in 1983
by Futura Publications, a Division of
Macdonald & Co (Publishers) Ltd
London & Sydney

This edition published by arrangement with Ballantine
Books, A Division of Random House, Inc.

ISBN 0 7088 2392 0

Reproduced, printed and bound in Great Britain by
Hazell Watson & Viney Ltd, Aylesbury, Bucks

Cover art and insert supplied by
Lucasfilm Ltd. (LFL.)

Futura Publications
A Division of
Macdonald & Co (Publishers) Ltd
Maxwell House
74 Worship Street
London EC2A 2EN

□ prologue

THE very depth of space. There was the length, and width, and height; and then these dimensions curved over on themselves into a bending blackness measurable only by the glinting stars that tumbled through the chasm, receding to infinity. To the very depth.

These stars marked the moments of the universe. There were aging orange embers, blue dwarfs, twin yellow giants. There were collapsing neutron stars, and angry supernovae that hissed into the icy emptiness. There were borning stars, breathing stars, pulsing stars, and dying stars. There was the Death Star.

At the feathered edge of the galaxy, the Death Star floated in stationary orbit above the green moon Endor—a moon whose mother planet had long since died of unknown cataclysm and disappeared into unknown realms. The Death Star was the Empire's armored battle station, nearly twice as big as its predecessor, which Rebel forces had destroyed so many years before— nearly twice as big, but more than twice as powerful. Yet it was only half complete.

Half a steely dark orb, it hung above the green world of Endor, tentacles of unfinished superstructure curling away toward its living companion like the groping legs of a deadly spider.

An Imperial Star Destroyer approached the giant space station at cruising speed. It was massive—a city itself—yet it moved with deliberate grace, like some great sea dragon. It was accompanied by dozens of Twin Ion Engine fighters—black insectlike combat flyers that zipped back and forth around the battleship's perimeter: scouting, sounding, docking, regrouping.

Soundlessly the main bay of the ship opened. There was a brief ignition-flash, as an Imperial shuttle emerged from the darkness of the hold, into the darkness of space. It sped toward the half-completed Death Star with quiet purpose.

In the cockpit the shuttle captain and his copilot made final readings, monitored descent functions. It was a sequence they'd each performed a thousand times, yet there was an unusual tension in the air now. The captain flipped the transmitter switch, and spoke into his mouthpiece.

"Command Station, this is ST321. Code Clearance Blue. We're starting our approach. Deactivate the security shield."

Static filtered over the receiver; then the voice of the port controller: "The security deflector shield will be deactivated when we have confirmation of your code transmission. Stand by…"

Once more silence filled the cockpit. The shuttle captain bit the inside of his cheek, smiled nervously at his copilot, and muttered, "Quick as you can, please—this better not take long. He's in no mood to wait…"

They refrained from glancing back into the passenger section of the shuttle, now under lights-out for landing. The unmistakable sound of the mechanical breathing coming from the chamber's shadow filled the cabin with a terrible impatience.

In the control room of the Death Star below, operators moved along the bank of panels, monitoring all the space traffic in the area, authorizing flight patterns, accessing certain areas to certain vehicles. The shield operator suddenly checked his monitor with alarm; the view-screen depicted the battle station itself, the moon Endor, and a web of energy—the deflector shield—emanating from the green moon, encompassing the Death Star. Only now, the security web was beginning to separate, to retract and form a clear channel—a channel through which the dot that was the Imperial shuttle sailed, unimpeded, toward the massive space station.

The shield operator quickly called his control officer over to the view-screen, uncertain how to proceed.

"What is it?" the officer demanded.

"That shuttle has a class-one priority ranking." He tried to replace the fear in his voice with disbelief.

The officer glanced at the view-screen for only a moment before realizing who was on the shuttle and spoke to himself: "Vader!"

He strode past the view port, where the shuttle could be seen already making its final approach, and headed toward the docking bay. He turned to the controller.

"Inform the commander that Lord Vader's shuttle has arrived."

The shuttle sat quietly, dwarfed by the cavernous reaches of the huge docking bay. Hundreds of troops stood assembled in formation, flanking the base of the shuttle ramp—white-armored Imperial stormtroopers, gray-suited officers, and the elite, red-robed Imperial Guard. They snapped to attention as Moff Jerjerrod entered.

Jerjerrod—tall, thin, arrogant—was the Death Star commander. He walked without hurry up the ranks of soldiers, to the ramp of the shuttle. Hurry was not in Jerjerrod, for hurry implied a wanting to be elsewhere, and he was a man who distinctively *was* exactly where he wanted to be. Great men never hurried (he was fond of saying); great men caused *others* to hurry.

Yet Jerjerrod was not blind to ambition; and a visit by such a one as this great Dark Lord could not be taken too lightly. He stood at the shuttle mouth, there-fore, waiting—with respect, but not hurry.

Suddenly the exit hatch of the shuttle opened, pull-ing the troops in formation to even tauter attention. Only darkness glowed from the exit at first; then foot-steps; then the characteristic electrical respirations, like the breathing of a machine; and finally Darth Vader, Lord of the Sith, emerged from the void.

Vader strode down the ramp, looking over the as-semblage. He stopped when he came to Jerjerrod. The commander bowed from the neck, and smiled.

"Lord Vader, this is an unexpected pleasure. We are honored by your presence."

"We can dispense with the pleasantries, Com-mander." Vader's words echoed as from the bottom of a well. "The Emperor is concerned with your progress. I am here to put you back on schedule."

Jerjerrod turned pale. This was news he'd not ex-pected. "I assure you, Lord Vader, my men are working as fast as they can."

"Perhaps I can encourage their progress in ways you have not considered," Vader growled. He had ways, of course; this was known. Ways, and ways again.

Jerjerrod kept his tone even, though deep inside, the ghost of hurry began to scrabble at his throat. "That won't be necessary, my Lord. I tell you, without ques-tion this station will be operational as planned."

"I'm afraid the Emperor does not share your opti-mistic appraisal of the situation."

"I fear he asks the impossible," the commander sug-gested.

"Perhaps you could explain that to him when he arrives." Vader's face remained invisible behind the deathly black mask that protected him; but the malice was clear in the electronically modified voice.

Jerjerrod's pallor intensified. "The Emperor is com-ing here?"

"Yes, Commander. And he will be quite displeased if you are still behind schedule when he arrives." He spoke loudly, to spread the threat over all who could hear.

"We shall double our efforts, Lord Vader." And he meant it. For sometimes didn't even great men hurry, in time of great need?

Vader lowered his voice again. "I hope so, Commander, for your sake. The Emperor will tolerate no further delay in the final destruction of the outlaw Rebellion. And we have secret news now"—he included Jerjerrod, only, in this intimate detail—"The Rebel fleet has gathered all its forces into a single giant armada. The time is at hand when we can crush them, without mercy, in a single blow."

For the briefest second, Vader's breathing seemed to quicken, then resumed its measured pace, like the rising of a hollow wind.

 1

OUTSIDE the small adobe hut, the sandstorm wailed like a beast in agony, refusing to die. Inside, the sounds were muted.

It was cooler in this shelter, more hushed, and darker. While the beast without howled, in this place of nuance and shadow a shrouded figure worked.

Tanned hands, holding arcane tools, extended from the sleeves of a caftanlike robe. The figure crouched on the ground, working. Before him lay a discoid device of strange design, wires trailing from it at one end, symbols etched into its flat surface. He connected the wired end to a tubular, smooth handle, pulled through an organic-looking connector, locked it in place with another tool. He motioned to a shadow in the corner; the shadow moved toward him.

Tentatively, the obscure form rolled closer to the robed figure. "Vrrrr-dit dweet?" the little R2 unit questioned timidly as it approached, pausing when it was just a foot from the shrouded man with the strange device.

The shrouded man motioned the droid nearer still. Artoo-Detoo scooted the last distance, blinking; and the hands raised toward his domed little head.

The fine sand blew hard over the dunes of Tatooine. The wind seemed to come from everywhere at once, typhooning in spots, swirling in devil-winds here, hovering in stillness there, without pattern or meaning.

A road wound across the desert plain. Its nature changed constantly, at one moment obscured by drifts of ochre sand, the next moment swept clean, or distorted by the heat of the shimmering air above it. A road more ephemeral than navigable; yet a road to be followed, all the same. For it was the only way to reach the palace of Jabba the Hutt.

Jabba was the vilest gangster in the galaxy. He had his fingers in smuggling, slave-trading, murder; his minions scattered across the stars. He both collected and invented atrocities, and his court was a den of unparalleled decay. It was said by some that Jabba had chosen Tatooine as his place of residence because only in this arid crucible of a planet could he hope to keep his soul from rotting away altogether—here the parched sun might bake his humor to a festering brine.

In any case, it was a place few of kind spirit even knew of, let alone approached. It was a place of evil, where even the most courageous felt their powers wilt under the foul gaze of Jabba's corruption.

"Poot-wEEt beDOO gung ooble DEEp!" vocalized Artoo-Detoo.

"Of course I'm worried," See-Threepio fussed. "And you should be too. Poor Lando Calrissian never returned from this place. Can you imagine what they've done to him?"

Artoo whistled timidly.

The golden droid waded stiffly through a shifting sand hill, then stopped short, as Jabba's palace suddenly loomed, suddenly dark, in the near distance. Artoo almost bumped into him, quickly skidding to the side of the road.

"Watch where you're going, Artoo." See-Threepio resumed walking, but more slowly, his little friend rolling along at his side. And as they went, he chattered on. "Why couldn't Chewbacca have delivered this message? No, whenever there's an impossible mission, they turn to us. No one worries about droids. Sometimes I wonder why we put up with it all."

On and on he rambled, over the desolate final stretch of road, until at last they reached the gates to the palace: massive iron doors, taller than Threepio could see—part of a series of stone and iron walls, forming several gigantic cylindrical towers that seemed to rise out of a mountain of packed sand.

The two droids fearfully looked around the ominous door for signs of life, or welcome, or some sort of signaling device with which to make their presence known. Seeing nothing in any of those categories, See-Threepio mustered his resolve (which function had been programmed into him quite a long time earlier), knocked softly three times on the thick metal gate, then quickly turned around and announced to Artoo, "There doesn't seem to be anyone here. Let's go back and tell Master Luke."

Suddenly a small hatch opened in the center of the door. A spindly mechanical arm popped out, affixed to which a large electronic eyeball peered unabashedly at the two droids. The eyeball spoke.

"Tee chuta hhat yudd!"

Threepio stood erect, proud though his circuits quivered a bit. He faced the eye, pointed to Artoo, and then to himself. "Artoo Detoowha bo Seethreepiosha ey toota odd mischka Jabba du Hutt."

The eye looked quickly from one robot to the other, then retracted back through the little window and slammed the hatch shut.

"Boo-dEEp gaNOOng," whispered Artoo with concern.

Threepio nodded. "I don't think they're going to let us in, Artoo. We'd better go." He turned to leave, as Artoo beeped a reluctant four-tone.

At that, a horrific, grinding screech erupted, and the massive iron door slowly began to rise. The two droids looked at each other skeptically, and then into the yawning black cavity that faced them. They waited, afraid to enter, afraid to retreat.

From the shadows, the strange voice of the eye screamed at them: "Nudd chaa!"

Artoo beeped and rolled forward into the gloom. Threepio hesitated, then rushed after his stubby companion with a start. "Artoo wait for me!" They stopped together in the gaping passageway, as Threepio scolded: "You'll get lost."

The great door slammed shut behind them with a monumental crash that echoed through the dark cavern. For a moment the two frightened robots stood there without moving; then, haltingly, they stepped forward.

They were immediately joined by three large Gamorrean guards—powerful piglike brutes whose racial hatred of robots was well known. The guards ushered the two droids down the dark corridor without so much as a nod. When they reached the first half-lit hallway, one of them grunted an order. Artoo beeped a nervous query at Threepio.

"You don't want to know," the golden droid responded apprehensively. "Just deliver Master Luke's message and get us out of here quick."

Before they could take another step, a form approached them from the obscurity of a cross-corridor: Bib Fortuna, the inelegant major-domo of Jabba's degenerate court. He was a tall, humanoid creature with eyes that saw only what was necessary, and a robe that hid all. Protruding from the back of his skull were two fat, tentacular appendages that exhibited prehensile, sensual, and cognitive functions at various times— which he wore either draped over his shoulders for decorative effect or, when the situation called for balance, hanging straight down behind him as if they were twin tails.

He smiled thinly as he stopped before the two robots. "Die wanna wanga."

Threepio spoke up officially. "Die wanna wanaga. We bring a message to your master, Jabba the Hutt." Artoo beeped a postscript, upon which Threepio nodded and added: "And a gift." He thought about this a moment, looked as puzzled as it was possible for a droid to look, and whispered loudly to Artoo, "Gift, what gift?"

Bib shook his head emphatically. "Nee Jabba no badda. Me chaade su goodie." He held out his hand toward Artoo.

The small droid backed up meekly, but his protest was lengthy. "bDooo EE NGrwrrr Op dbooDEEop!"

"Artoo, give it to him!" Threepio insisted. Sometimes Artoo could be *so* binary.

At this, though, Artoo became positively defiant, beeping and tooting at Fortuna and Threepio as if they'd *both* had their programs erased.

Threepio nodded finally, hardly happy with Artoo's answer. He smiled apologetically at Bib. "He says our master's instructions are to give it only to Jabba himself." Bib considered the problem a moment, as Threepio went on explaining. "I'm terribly sorry. I'm afraid he's ever so stubborn about these things." He managed to throw a disparaging yet loving tone into his voice, as he tilted his head toward his small associate.

Bib gestured for them to follow. "Nudd chaa." He walked back into the darkness, the droids following close behind, the three Gamorrean guards lumbering along at the rear.

As See-Threepio descended into the belly of the shadow, he muttered quietly to the silent R2 unit, "Artoo, I have a bad feeling about this."

See-Threepio and Artoo-Detoo stood at the entrance of the throne room, looking in. "We're doomed," whimpered Threepio, wishing for the thousandth time that he could close his eyes.

The room was filled, wall to cavernous wall, with the animate dregs of the universe. Grotesque creatures from the lowest star systems, drunk on spiced liquor and their own fetid vapors. Gamorreans, twisted humans, jawas—all reveling in base pleasures, or raucously comparing mean feats. And at the front of the room, reclining on a daïs that overlooked the debauchery, was Jabba the Hutt.

His head was three times human size, perhaps four. His eyes were yellow, reptilian—his skin was like a snake's, as well, except covered with a fine layer of grease. He had no neck, but only a series of chins that expanded finally into a great bloated body, engorged to bursting with stolen morsels. Stunted, almost useless arms sprouted from his upper torso, the sticky fingers of his left hand languidly wrapped around the smoking-end of his water-pipe. He had no hair—it had fallen out from a combination of diseases. He had no legs—his trunk simply tapered gradually to a long, plump snake-tail that stretched along the length of the platform like a tube of yeasty dough. His lipless mouth was wide, almost ear to ear, and he drooled continuously. He was quite thoroughly disgusting.

Chained to him, chained at the neck, was a sad, pretty dancing-girl, a member of Fortuna's species, with two dry, shapely tentacles sprouting from the back of her head, hanging suggestively down her bare, muscled back. Her name was Oola. Looking forlorn, she sat as far away as her chain would allow, at the other end of the daïs.

And sitting near Jabba's belly was a small monkey-like reptile named Salacious Crumb, who caught all the food and ooze that spilled out of Jabba's hands or mouth and ate it with a nauseating cackle.

Shafts of light from above partially illuminated the drunken courtiers as Bib Fortuna crossed the floor to the daïs. The room was composed of an endless series of alcoves within alcoves, so that much of what went on was, in any case, visible only as shadow and movement. When Fortuna reached the throne, he delicately leaned forward and whispered into the slobbering monarch's ear. Jabba's eyes became slits...then with a maniacal laugh he motioned for the two terrified droids to be brought in.

"Bo shuda," wheezed the Hutt, and lapsed into a fit of coughing. Although he understood several languages, as a point of honor he only spoke Huttese. His only such point.

The quaking robots scooted forward to stand before the repulsive ruler, though he grossly violated their most deeply programmed sensibilities. "The message, Artoo, the message," Threepio urged.

Artoo whistled once, and a beam of light projected from his domed head, creating a hologram of Luke Skywalker that stood before them on the floor. Quickly the image grew to over ten feet tall, until the young Jedi warrior towered over the assembled throng. All at once the room grew quiet, as Luke's giant presence made itself felt.

"Greetings, Exalted One," the hologram said to Jabba. "Allow me to introduce myself. I am Luke Skywalker, Jedi Knight and friend of Captain Solo. I seek an audience with Your Greatness, to bargain for his life." At this, the entire room burst into laughter which Jabba instantly stopped with a hand motion. Luke didn't pause long. "I know that you are powerful, mighty Jabba, and that your anger with Solo must be equally powerful. But I'm sure we can work out an arrangement which will be mutually beneficial. As a token of my good will, I present to you a gift—these two droids."

Threepio jumped back as if stung. "What! What did he say?"

Luke continued. "...Both are hardworking and will serve you well." With that, the hologram disappeared.

Threepio wagged his head in despair. "Oh no, this can't be. Artoo, you must have played the wrong message."

Jabba laughed and drooled.

Bib spoke in Huttese. "Bargain rather than fight? He is no Jedi."

Jabba nodded in agreement. Still grinning, he rasped at Threepio, "There will be no bargain. I have no intention of giving up my favorite decoration." With a hideous chuckle he looked toward the dimly lit alcove beside the throne; there, hanging flat against the wall, was the carbonized form of Han Solo, his face and hands emerging out of the cold hard slab, like a statue reaching from a sea of stone.

Artoo and Threepio marched dismally through the dank passageway at the prodding of a Gamorrean guard. Dungeon cells lined both walls. The unspeakable cries of anguish that emanated from within as the droids passed echoed off the stone and down the endless catacombs. Periodically a hand or claw or tentacle would reach through the bars of a door to grab at the hapless robots.

Artoo beeped pitifully. Threepio only shook his head. "What could have possibly come over Master Luke? Was it something I did? He never expressed any unhappiness with my work..."

They approached a door at the end of the corridor. It slid open automatically, and the Gamorrean shoved them foward. Inside, their ears were assaulted by deafening machine sounds—wheels creaking, piston-heads slamming, water-hammers, engine hums—and a continuously shifting haze of steam made visibility short. This was either the boiler room, or programmed hell.

An agonized electronic scream, like the sound of stripping gears, drew their attention to the corner of the room. From out of the mist walked EV-9D9, a thin humanlike robot with some disturbingly human appetites. In the dimness behind Ninedenine, Threepio could see the legs being pulled off a droid on a torture rack, while a second droid, hanging upside down, was having red-hot irons applied to its feet; it had emitted the electronic scream Threepio heard a few moments earlier, as the sensor circuits in its metal skin melted in agony. Threepio cringed at the sound, his own wiring sympathetically crackling with static electricity.

Ninedenine stopped in front of Threepio, raising her pincer hands expansively. "Ah, new acquisitions," she said with great satisfaction. "I am Eve-Ninedenine, Chief of Cyborg Operations. You're a protocol droid, aren't you?"

"I am See-Threepio, human-cyborg re—"

"Yes or no will do," Ninedenine said icily.

"Well, yes," Threepio replied. This robot was going to be trouble, that much was obvious—one of those droids who always had to prove she was more-droid-than-thou.

"How many languages do you speak?" Ninedenine continued.

Well, two can play at that game, thought Threepio. He ran his most dignified, official introductory tape. "I am fluent in over six million forms of communication, and can—"

"Splendid!" Ninedenine interrupted gleefully. "We have been without an interpreter since the master got angry with something our last protocol droid said and disintegrated him."

"Disintegrated!" Threepio wailed. Any semblance of protocol left him.

Ninedenine spoke to a pig guard who suddenly appeared. "This one will be quite useful. Fit him with a restraining bolt, then take him back up to the main audience chamber."

The guard grunted and roughly shoved Threepio toward the door.

"Artoo, don't leave me!" Threepio called out, but the guard grabbed him and pulled him away; and he was gone.

Artoo let out a long, plaintive cry as Threepio was removed. Then he turned to Ninedenine and beeped in outrage, and at length.

Ninedenine laughed. "You're a feisty little one, but you'll soon learn some respect. I have need for you on the master's Sail Barge. Several of our astrodroids have been disappearing recently—stolen for spare parts, most likely. I think you'll fill in nicely."

The droid on the torture rack emitted a high-frequency wail, then sparked briefly and was silent.

The court of Jabba the Hutt roiled in malignant ecstasy. Oola, the beautiful creature chained to Jabba, danced in the center of the floor, as the inebriated monsters cheered and heckled. Threepio hovered warily near the back of the throne, trying to keep the lowest profile possible. Periodically he had to duck to avoid a fruit hurled in his direction or to sidestep a rolling body. Mostly, he just stayed low. What else was a protocol droid to do, in a place of so little protocol?

Jabba leered through the smoke of his hooka and beckoned the creature Oola to come sit beside him. She stopped dancing instantly, a fearful look in her eye, and backed up, shaking her head. Apparently she had suffered such invitations before.

Jabba became angry. He pointed unmistakably to a spot beside him on the daïs. "Da eitha!" he growled.

Oola shook her head more violently, her face a mask of terror. "Na chuba negatorie. Na! Na! Natoota..."

Jabba became livid. Furiously he motioned to Oola. "Boscka!"

Jabba pushed a button as he released Oola's chain. Before she could flee, a grating trap door in the floor dropped open, and she tumbled into the pit below. The door snapped shut instantly. A moment of silence, followed by a low, rumbling roar, followed by a terrified shriek was followed once more by silence.

Jabba laughed until he slobbered. A dozen revelers hurried over to peer through the grate, to observe the demise of the nubile dancer.

Threepio shrank even lower and looked for support to the carbonite form of Han Solo, suspended in bas relief above the floor. Now *there* was a human without a sense of protocol, thought Threepio wistfully.

His reverie was interrupted by an unnatural quiet that suddenly fell over the room. He looked up to see

Bib Fortuna making his way through the crowd, accompanied by two Gamorrean guards, and followed by a fierce-looking cloaked-and-helmeted bounty hunter who led his captive prize on a leash: Chewbacca, the Wookiee.

Threepio gasped, stunned. "Oh, no! Chewbacca!" The future was looking very bleak indeed.

Bib muttered a few words into Jabba's ear, pointing to the bounty hunter and his captive. Jabba listened intently. The bounty hunter was humanoid, small and mean: a belt of cartridges was slung across his jerkin and an eye-slit in his helmet-mask gave the impression of his being able to see through things. He bowed low, then spoke in fluent Ubese. "Greetings, Majestic One. I am Boushh." It was a metallic language, well-adapted to the rarefied atmosphere of the home planet from which this nomadic species arose.

Jabba answered in the same tongue, though his Ubese was stilted and slow. "At last someone has brought me the mighty Chewbacca..." He tried to continue, but stuttered on the word he wanted. With a roaring laugh, he turned toward Threepio. "Where's my talkdroid?" he boomed, motioning Threepio to come closer. Reluctantly, the courtly robot obeyed.

Jabba ordered him congenially. "Welcome our mercenary friend and ask his price for the Wookiee."

Threepio translated the message to the bounty hunter. Boushh listened carefully, simultaneously studying the feral creatures around the room, possible exits, possible hostages, vulnerable points. He particularly noticed Boba Fett—standing near the door—the steel-masked mercenary who had caught Han Solo.

Boushh assessed this all in a moment's moment, then spoke evenly in his native tongue to Threepio. "I will take fifty thousand, no less."

Threepio quietly translated for Jabba, who immediately became enraged and knocked the golden droid off the raised throne with a sweep of his massive tail. Threepio clattered in a heap on the floor, where he rested momentarily, uncertain of the correct protocol in this situation.

Jabba raved on in gutteral Huttese, Boushh shifted his weapon to a more usable position. Threepio sighed, struggled back onto the throne, composed himself, and translated for Boushh—loosely—what Jabba was saying.

"Twenty-five thousand is all he'll pay..." Threepio instructed.

Jabba motioned his pig guards to take Chewbacca, as two jawas covered Boushh. Boba Fett, also raised his weapon. Jabba added, to Threepio's translation: "Twenty five thousand, plus his life."

Threepio translated. The room was silent, tense, uncertain. Finally Boushh spoke, softly, to Threepio.

"Tell that swollen garbage bag he'll have to do better than that, or they'll be picking his smelly hide out of every crack in this room. I'm holding a thermal detonator."

Threepio suddenly focused on the small silver ball Boushh held partially concealed in his left hand. It could be heard humming a quiet, ominous hum. Threepio looked nervously at Jabba, then back at Boushh.

Jabba barked at the droid. "Well? What did he say?"

Threepio cleared his throat. "Your Grandness, he, uh...He—"

"Out with it, droid!" Jabba roared.

"Oh, dear," Threepio fretted. He inwardly prepared himself for the worst, then spoke to Jabba in flawless Huttese. "Boushh respectfully disagrees with Your Exaltedness, and begs you to reconsider the amount...or he will release the thermal detonator he is holding."

Instantly a disturbed murmuring circled in the room. Everyone backed up several feet, as if that would help. Jabba stared at the ball clenched in the bounty hunter's hand. It was beginning to glow. Another tense hush came over the onlookers.

Jabba stared malevolently at the bounty hunter for several long seconds. Then, slowly, a satisfied grin crept over his vast, ugly mouth. From the bilious pit of his belly, a laugh rose like gas in a mire. "This bounty hunter is my kind of scum. Fearless and inventive. Tell him thirty-five, no more—and warn him not to press his luck."

Threepio felt greatly relieved by this turn of events. He translated for Boushh. Everyone studied the bounty hunter closely for his reaction; guns were readied.

Then Boushh released a switch on the thermal detonator, and it went dead. "Zeebuss," he nodded.

"He agrees," Threepio said to Jabba.

The crowd cheered; Jabba relaxed. "Come, my friend, join our celebration. I may find other work for you." Threepio translated, as the party resumed in depraved revelry.

Chewbacca growled under his breath, as he was led away by the Gamorreans. He might have cracked their heads just for being so ugly, or to remind everyone present what a Wookiee was made of—but near the door he spotted a familiar face. Hidden behind a half-mask of pit-boar teeth was a human in the uniform of a skiff guard—Lando Calrissian. Chewbacca gave no sign of recognition; nor did he resist the guard who now escorted him from the room.

Lando had managed to infiltrate this nest of maggots months earlier to see if it was possible to free Solo from Jabba's imprisonment. He'd done this for several reasons.

First, because he felt (correctly) that it was his fault Han was in this predicament, and he wanted to make amends—provided, of course, he could do so without getting hurt. Blending in here, like just one of the pirates, was no problem for Lando, though—mistaken identity was a way of life with him.

Second, he wanted to join forces with Han's buddies at the top of the Rebel Alliance. They were out to beat the Empire, and he wanted nothing more in his life now than to do just that. The Imperial police had moved in on his action once too often; so this was a grudge match, now. Besides, Lando liked being part of Solo's crowd, since they seemed to be right up at the business end of all the action against the Empire.

Third, Princess Leia had asked him to help, and he just never could refuse a princess asking for help. Besides, you never knew how she might thank you some day.

Finally, Lando would have bet anything that Han simply could not be rescued from this place—and Lando just plain couldn't resist a bet.

So he spent his days watching a lot. Watching and calculating. That's what he did now, as Chewie was led away—he watched, and then he faded into the stonework.

The band started playing, led by a blue, flop-eared jizz-wailer named Max Rebo. Dancers flooded the floor. The courtiers hooted, and brewed their brains a bit more.

Boushh leaned against a column, surveying the scene. His gaze swept coolly over the court, taking in the dancers, the smokers, the rollers, the gamblers...until it came to rest squarely on an equally unflappable stare from across the room. Boba Fett was watching him.

Boushh shifted slightly, posturing with his weapon cradled like a loving child. Boba Fett remained motionless, an arrogant sneer all but visible behind his ominous mask.

Pig guards led Chewbacca though the unlit dungeon corridor. A tentacle coiled out one of the doors to touch the brooding Wookiee.

"Rheeaaahhr!" he screamed, and the tentacle shot back into its cell.

The next door was open. Before Chewie fully realized what was happening, he was hurled forcefully into the cell by all the guards. The door slammed shut, locking him in darkness.

He raised his head and let out a long, pitiful howl

that carried through the entire mountain of iron and sand up to the infinitely patient sky.

The throne room was quiet, dark, and empty as night filled its littered corners. Blood, wine, and saliva stained the floor, shreds of tattered clothing hung from the fixtures, unconscious bodies curled under broken furniture. The party was over.

A dark figure moved silently among the shadows, pausing behind a column here, a statue there. He made his way stealthily along the perimeter of the room, stepping once over a snoring Yak Face. He never made a sound. This was Boushh, the bounty hunter.

He reached the curtained alcove beside which the slab that was Han Solo hung suspended by a force field on the wall. Boushh looked around furtively, then flipped a switch near the side of the carbonite coffin. The humming of the force field wound down, and the heavy monolith slowly lowered to the floor.

Boushh stepped up and studied the frozen face of the space pirate. He touched Solo's carbonized cheek, curiously, as if it were a rare, precious stone. Cold and hard as diamond.

For a few seconds he examined the controls at the side of the slab, then activated a series of switches. Finally, after one last, hesitant, glance at the living statue before him, he slid the decarbonization lever into place.

The casing began to emit a high-pitched sound. Anxiously Boushh peered all around again, making certain no one heard. Slowly, the hard shell that was covering the contours of Solo's face started to melt away. Soon, the coating was gone from the entire front of Solo's body, freeing his upraised hands—so long frozen in protest—to fall slackly to his sides. His face relaxed into what looked like nothing so much as a death-mask. Boushh extracted the lifeless body from its casing and lowered it gently to the floor.

He leaned his gruesome helmet close to Solo's face, listening closely for signs of life. No breath. No pulse.

With a start, Han's eyes suddenly snapped open, and he began to cough. Boushh steadied him, tried to quiet him—there were still guards who might hear.

"Quiet!" he whispered. "Just relax."

Han squinted up at the dim form above him. "I can't see…What's happening?" He was, understandably, disoriented, after having been in suspended animation for six of this desert planet's months—a period that was, to him, timeless. It had been a grim sensation—as if for an eternity he'd been trying to draw breath, to move, to scream, every moment in conscious, painful asphyxiation—and now suddenly he was dumped into a loud, black, cold pit.

His senses assaulted him all at once. The air bit at his skin with a thousand icy teeth; the opacity of his sight was impenetrable; wind seemed to rush around his ears at hurricane volumes; he couldn't feel which way was up; the myriad smells filling his nose made him nauseous, he couldn't stop salivating, all his bones hurt—and then came the visions.

Visions from his childhood, from his last breakfast, from twenty-seven piracies…as if all the images and memories of his life had been crammed into a balloon, and the balloon popped and they all came bursting out now, randomly, in a single moment. It was nearly overwhelming, it was sensory overload; or more precisely, memory overload. Men had gone mad, in these first minutes following decarbonization, hopelessly, utterly mad—unable ever again to reorganize the ten-billion individual images that comprised a lifespan into any kind of coherent, selective order.

Solo wasn't that susceptible. He rode the surge of this tide of impressions until it settled down to a churning backwash, submerging the bulk of his memories, leaving only the most recent flotsam to foam on the surface: his betrayal by Lando Calrissian, whom he'd once called friend; his ailing ship; his last view of Leia; his capture by Boba Fett, the iron-masked bounty hunter who…

Where was he now? What had happened? His last

image was of Boba Fett watching him turn into carbonite. Was this Fett again now, come to thaw him for more abuse? The air roared in his ears, his breathing felt irregular, unnatural. He batted his hand in front of his face.

Boushh tried to reassure him. "You're free of the carbonite and have hibernation sickness. Your eyesight will return in time. Come, we must hurry if we're to leave this place."

Reflexively Han grabbed the bounty hunter, felt at the grated face-mask, then drew back. "I'm not going anywhere—I don't even know where I am." He began sweating profusely as his heart once again churned blood, and his mind groped for answers. "Who are you, anyway?" he demanded suspiciously. Perhaps it was Fett after all.

The bounty hunter reached up and pulled the helmet away from his head revealing, underneath, the beautiful face of Princess Leia.

"One who loves you," she whispered, taking his face tenderly in her still-gloved hands and kissing him long on the lips.

 2

HAN strained to see her, though he had the eyes of a newborn. "Leia! Where are we?"

"Jabba's palace. I've got to get you out of here quick."

He sat up shakily. "Everything's a blur...I'm not going to be much help..."

She looked at him a long moment, her blinded love—she'd traveled light-years to find him, risked her life, lost hard-won time needed sorely by the Rebellion, time she couldn't really afford to throw away on personal quests and private desires...but she loved him.

Tears filled her eyes. "We'll make it," she whispered.

Impulsively, she embraced him and kissed him again. He, too, was flooded with emotion all at once—back from the dead, the beautiful princess filling his arms, snatching him from the teeth of the void. He felt overwhelmed. Unable to move, even to speak, he held her tightly, his blind eyes closed fast against all the sordid realities that would come rushing in soon enough.

Sooner than that, as it happened. A repulsive squish-
ing sound suddenly became all too obvious behind
them. Han opened his eyes, but could still see nothing.
Leia looked up to the alcove beyond, and her gaze
turned to an expression of horror. For the curtain had
been drawn away, and the entire area, floor to ceiling,
was composed of a gallery of the most disgusting mis-
creants of Jabba's court—gawking, salivating, wheez-
ing.

Leia's hand shot up to her mouth.

"What is it?" Han pressed her. Something obviously
was terribly wrong. He stared into his own blackness.

An obscene cackle rose from the other side of the
alcove. A Huttese cackle.

Han held his head, closed his eyes again, as if to
keep away the inevitable for just one more moment.
"I know that laugh."

The curtain on the far side was suddenly drawn
open. There sat Jabba, Ishi Tib, Bib, Boba, and several
guards. They all laughed, kept laughing, laughed to
punish.

"My, my, what a touching sight," Jabba purred. "Han,
my boy, your taste in companions has improved, even
if your luck has not."

Even blind, Solo could slide into smooth talk easier
than a spice-eater. "Listen, Jabba, I was on my way
back to pay you when I got a little side-tracked. Now
I know we've had our differences, but I'm sure we can
work this out..."

This time Jabba genuinely chuckled. "It's too late
for that, Solo. You may have been the best smuggler
in the business, but now you're Bantha fodder." He
cut short his smile and gestured to his guards. "Take
him."

Guards grabbed Leia and Han. They dragged the
Corellian pirate off, while Leia continued struggling
where she was.

"I will decide how to kill him later," Jabba muttered.

"I'll pay you triple," Solo called out. "Jabba, you're

throwing away a fortune. Don't be a fool." Then he was gone.

From the rank of guards, Lando quickly moved forward, took hold of Leia, and attempted to lead her away.

Jabba stopped them. "Wait! Bring her to me."

Lando and Leia halted in mid-stride. Lando looked tense, uncertain what to do. It wasn't quite time to move yet. The odds still weren't just right. He knew he was the ace-in-the-hole, and an ace-in-the-hole was something you had to know how to play to win.

"I'll be all right," Leia whispered.

"I'm not so sure," he replied. But the moment was past; there was nothing else to be done now. He and Ishi Tib, the Birdlizard, dragged the young princess to Jabba.

Threepio, who'd been watching everything from his place behind Jabba, could watch no more. He turned away in dread.

Leia, on the other hand, stood tall before the loathsome monarch. Her anger ran high. With all the galaxy at war, for her to be detained on this dustball of a planet by this petty scumdealer was more outrageous than she could tolerate. Still, she kept her voice calm; for she was, in the end, a princess. "We have powerful friends Jabba. You will soon regret this..."

"I'm sure, I'm sure," the old gangster rumbled with glee, "but in the meantime, I will thoroughly enjoy the pleasure of your company."

He pulled her eagerly to him until their faces were mere inches apart, her belly pressed to his oily snake skin. She thought about killing him outright, then and there. But she held her ire in check, since the rest of these vermin might have killed her before she could escape with Han. Better odds were sure to come later. So she swallowed hard and, for the time being, put up with this slimepot as best she could.

Threepio peeked out momentarily, then immediately withdrew again. "Oh no, I can't watch."

Foul beast that he was, Jabba poked his fat, dripping tongue out to the princess, and slopped a beastly kiss squarely on her mouth.

Han was thrown roughly into the dungeon cell; the door crashed shut behind him. He fell to the floor in the darkness, then picked himself up and sat against the wall. After a few moments of pounding the ground with his fist, he quieted down and tried to organize his thoughts.

Darkness. Well, blast it, blind is blind. No use wishing for moondew on a meteorite. Only it was so frustrating, coming out of deep-freeze like that, saved by the one person who...

Leia! The star captain's stomach dropped at the thought of what must be happening to her now. If only he knew where he was. Tentatively he knocked on the wall behind him. Solid rock.

What could he do? Bargain, maybe. But what did he have to bargain with? Dumb question, he thought— when did I ever have to *have* something before I could *bargain* with it?

What, though? Money? Jabba had more than he could ever count. Pleasures? Nothing could give Jabba more pleasure than to defile the princess and kill Solo. No, things were bad—in fact, it didn't look like they could get much worse.

Then he heard the growl. A low, formidable snarl from out of the dense blackness at the far corner of the cell, the growl of a large and angry beast.

The hair on Solo's arms stood on end. Quickly he rose, his back to the wall. "Looks like I've got company," he muttered.

The wild creature bellowed out an insane *"Groawwwwr!"* and raced straight at Solo, grabbing him ferociously around the chest, lifting him several feet into the air, squeezing off his breathing.

Han was totally motionless for several long seconds—he couldn't believe his ears. "Chewie, is that you!?"

The giant Wookiee barked with joy.

For the second time in an hour, Solo was overcome with happiness; but this was an entirely different matter. "All right, all right, wait a second, you're crushing me."

Chewbacca put his friend down. Han reached up and scratched his partner's chest; Chewie cooed like a pup.

"Okay, what's going on around here, anyway?" Han was instantly back on track. Here was unbelievably good fortune—here was someone he could make a plan *with*. And not only someone, but his most loyal friend in the galaxy.

Chewie filled him in at length. "Arh arhaghh shpahrgh rahr aurowwwrahrah grop rahp rah."

"Lando's plan? What is *he* doing here?"

Chewie barked extensively.

Han shook his head. "Is Luke crazy? Why'd you listen to him? That kid can't even take care of himself, let alone rescue anyone."

"Rowr ahrgh awf ahraroww rowh rohngr grgrff rf rf."

"A Jedi Knight? Come on. I'm out of it for a little while and everybody gets delusions…"

Chewbacca growled insistently.

Han nodded dubiously in the blackness. "I'll believe it when I see it—" he commented, walking stoutly into the wall. "If you'll excuse the expression."

The iron main gate of Jabba's palace scraped open harshly, oiled only with sand and time. Standing outside in the dusty gale, staring into the black cavernous entranceway, was Luke Skywalker.

He was clad in the robe of the Jedi Knight—a cassock, really—but bore neither gun nor lightsaber. He stood loosely, without bravado, taking a measure of the place before entering. He was a man now. Wiser, like a man—older more from loss than from years. Loss of illusions, loss of dependency. Loss of friends, to war. Loss of sleep, to stress. Loss of laughter. Loss of his hand.

But of all his losses, the greatest was that which came from knowledge, and from the deep recognition that he could never un-know what he knew. So many things he wished he'd never learned. He had aged with the weight of this knowledge.

Knowledge brought benefits, of course. He was less impulsive now. Manhood had given him perspective, a framework in which to fit the events of his life—that is, a lattice of spatial and time coordinates spanning his existence, back to earliest memories, ahead to a hundred alternative futures. A lattice of depths, and conundrums, and interstices, through which Luke could peer at any new event in his life, peer at it with perspective. A lattice of shadows and corners, rolling back to the vanishing point on the horizon of Luke's mind. And all these shadow boxes that lent such *perspective* to things ... well, this lattice gave his life a certain darkness.

Nothing of substance, of course—and in any case, some would have said this shading gave a depth to his personality, where before it had been thin, without dimension—though such a suggestion probably would have come from jaded critics, reflecting a jaded time. Nonetheless, there was a certain darkness, now.

There were other advantages to knowledge: rationality, etiquette, choice. Choice, of them all, was a true double-edged sword; but it did have its advantages.

Furthermore he was skilled in the craft of the Jedi now, where before he'd been merely precocious.

He was more aware now.

These were all desirable attributes, to be sure; and Luke knew as well as anyone that all things alive must grow. Still, it carried a certain sadness, the sum of all this knowledge. A certain sense of regret. But who could afford to be a boy in times such as these?

Resolutely, Luke strode into the arching hallway.

Almost immediately two Gamorreans stepped up, blocking his path. One spoke in a voice that did not invite debate. "No chuba!"

Luke raised his hand and pointed at the guards. Before either could draw a weapon, they were both clutching their own throats, choking, gasping. They fell to their knees.

Luke lowered his hand and walked on. The guards, suddenly able to breathe again, slumped to the sand-drifted steps. They didn't follow.

Around the next corner Luke was met by Bib Fortuna. Fortuna began speaking as he approached the young Jedi, but Luke never broke stride, so Bib had to reverse his direction in mid-sentence and hurry along with Skywalker in order to carry on a conversation.

"You must be the one called Skywalker. His Excellency will not see you."

"I will speak to Jabba, now," Luke spoke evenly, never slowing. They passed several more guards at the next crossing, who fell in behind them.

"The great Jabba is asleep," Bib explained. "He has instructed me to tell you there will be no bargains—"

Luke stopped suddenly, and stared at Bib. He locked eyes with the major-domo, raised his hand slightly, took a minutely inward turn. "You will take me to Jabba, now."

Bib paused, tilted his head a fraction. What were his instructions? Oh, yes, now he remembered. "I will take you to Jabba now."

He turned and walked down the twisting corridor that led to the throne chamber. Luke followed him into the gloom.

"You serve your master well," he whispered in Bib's ear.

"I serve my master well," Bib nodded with conviction.

"You are sure to be rewarded," Luke added.

Bib smiled smugly. "I am sure to be rewarded."

As Luke and Bib entered Jabba's court, the level of tumult dropped precipitously as if Luke's presence had a cooling effect. Everyone felt the change.

The lieutenant and the Jedi Knight approached the

throne. Luke saw Leia seated there, now, by Jabba's belly. She was chained at the neck and dressed in the skimpy costume of a dancing girl. He could feel her pain immediately, from across the room—but he said nothing, didn't even look at her, shut her anguish completely out of his mind. For he needed to focus his attention entirely on Jabba.

Leia, for her part, sensed this at once. She closed her mind to Luke, to keep herself from distracting him; yet at the same time she kept it open, ready to receive any sliver of information she might need to act. She felt charged with possibilities.

Threepio peeked out from behind the throne as Bib walked up. For the first time in many days, he scanned his hope program. "Ah! At last Master Luke's come to take me away from all this," he beamed.

Bib stood proudly before Jabba. "Master, I present Luke Skywalker, Jedi Knight."

"I told you not to admit him," the gangster-slug growled in Huttese.

"I must be allowed to speak," Luke spoke quietly, though his words were heard throughout the hall.

"He must be allowed to speak," Bib concurred thoughtfully.

Jabba, furious, bashed Bib across the face and sent him reeling to the floor. "You weak-minded fool! He's using an old Jedi mind trick!"

Luke let all the rest of the motley horde that surrounded him melt into the recesses of his consciousness, to let Jabba fill his mind totally. "You will bring Captain Solo and the Wookiee to me."

Jabba smiled grimly. "Your mind powers will not work on me, boy. I am not affected by your human thought pattern." Then, as an afterthought: "I was killing your kind when being a Jedi meant something."

Luke altered his stance somewhat, internally and externally. "Nevertheless, I am taking Captain Solo and his friends. You can either profit from this...or be destroyed. It's your choice, but I warn you not to un-

derestimate my powers." He spoke in his own language, which Jabba well understood.

Jabba laughed the laugh of a lion cautioned by a
mouse.

Threepio, who had been observing this interplay
intently, leaned forward to whisper to Luke: "Master,
you're standing—" A guard abruptly restrained the
concerned droid, though, and pulled him back to his
place.

Jabba cut short his laugh with a scowl. "There will
be no bargain, young Jedi. I shall enjoy watching you
die."

Luke raised his hand. A pistol jumped out of the
holster of a nearby guard and landed snugly in the
Jedi's palm. Luke pointed the weapon at Jabba.

Jabba spat. "Boscka!"

The floor suddenly dropped away, sending Luke
and his guard crashing into the pit below. The trap
door immediately closed again. All the beasts of the
court rushed to the floor-grating and looked down.

"Luke!" yelled Leia. She felt part of her self torn
away, pulled down into the pit with him. She started
forward, but was held in check by the manacle around
her throat. Raucous laughter crowded in from everywhere at once, set her on edge. She poised to flee.

A human guard touched her shoulder. She looked.
It was Lando. Imperceptibly, he shook his head No.
Imperceptibly, her muscles relaxed. This wasn't the
right moment, he knew—but it was the right hand. All
the cards were here, now—Luke, Han, Leia, Chew-
bacca... and old Wild Card Lando. He just didn't want
Leia revealing the hand before all the bets were out.
The stakes were just too high.

In the pit below, Luke picked himself up off the
floor. He found he was now in a large cavelike dungeon, the walls formed of craggy boulders pocked with
lightless crevices. The half-chewed bones of countless
animals were strewn over the floor, smelling of decayed flesh and twisted fear.

Twenty-five feet above him, in the ceiling, he saw the iron grating through which Jabba's repugnant courtiers peered.

The guard beside him suddenly began to scream uncontrollably, as a door in the side of the cave slowly rumbled open. With infinite calm, Luke surveyed his surroundings as he removed his long robe down to his Jedi tunic, to give him more freedom of movement. He backed quickly to the wall and crouched there, watching.

Out of the side passage emerged the giant Rancor. The size of an elephant, it was somehow reptilian, somehow as unformed as a nightmare. Its huge screeching mouth was asymmetrical in its head, its fangs and claws set all out of proportion. It was clearly a mutant, and wild as all unreason.

The guard picked up the pistol from the dirt where it had fallen and began firing laser bursts at the hideous monster. This only made the beast angrier. It lumbered toward the guard.

The guard kept firing. Ignoring the laser blasts, the beast grabbed the hysterical guard, popped him into its slavering jaws, and swallowed him in a gulp. The audience above cheered, laughed, and threw coins.

The monster then turned and started for Luke. But the Jedi Knight leaped eight meters straight up and grabbed onto the overhead grate. The crowd began to boo. Hand over hand, Luke traversed the grating toward the corner of the cave, struggling to maintain his grip as the audience jeered his efforts. One hand slipped on the oily grid, and he dangled precariously over the baying mutant.

Two jawas ran across the top of the grate. They mashed Luke's fingers with their rifle butts; once again, the crowd roared its approval.

The Rancor pawed at Luke from below, but the Jedi dangled just out of reach. Suddenly Luke released his hold and dropped directly onto the eye of the howling monster; he then tumbled to the floor.

The Rancor screamed in pain and stumbled, swatting its own face to knock away the agony. It ran in circles a few times, then spotted Luke again and came at him. Luke stooped down to pick up the long bone of an earlier victim. He brandished it before him. The gallery above thought this was hilarious and hooted in delight.

The monster grabbed Luke and brought him up to its salivating mouth. At the last moment, though, Luke wedged the bone deep in the Rancor's mouth and jumped to the floor as the beast began to gag. The Rancor bellowed and flailed about, running headlong into a wall. Several rocks were dislodged, starting an avalanche that nearly buried Luke, as he crouched deep in a crevice near the floor. The crowd clapped in unison.

Luke tried to clear his mind. Fear is a great cloud, Ben used to tell him. It makes the cold colder and the dark darker; but let it rise and it will dissolve. So Luke let it rise past the clamor of the beast above him, and examined ways he might turn the sad creature's rantings on itself.

It was not an evil beast, that much was clear. Had it been purely malicious, its wickedness could easily have been turned on itself—for pure evil, Ben had said, was always self-destructive in the end. But this monster wasn't bad—merely dumb and mistreated. Hungry and in pain, it lashed out at whatever came near. For Luke to have looked on that as evil would only have been a projection of Luke's own darker aspects—it would have been false, and it certainly wouldn't have helped him out of this situation.

No, he was going to have to keep his mind clear—that was all—and just outwit the savage brute, to put it out of its misery.

Most preferable would have been to set it loose in Jabba's court, but that seemed unlikely. He considered, next, giving the creature the means to do itself in—to end its own pain. Unfortunately, the creature was far too angered to comprehend the solace of the void. Luke finally began studying the specific contours of the cave, to try to come up with a specific plan.

The Rancor, meanwhile, had knocked the bone from its mouth and, enraged, was scrabbling through the rubble of fallen rocks, searching for Luke. Luke, though his vision was partially obscured by the pile that still sheltered him, could see now past the monster, to a holding cave beyond—and beyond that, to a utility door. If only he could get to it.

The Rancor knocked away a boulder and spotted Luke recoiling in the crevice. Voraciously, it reached in to pluck the boy out. Luke grabbed a large rock and smashed it down on the creature's finger as hard as he could. As the Rancor jumped, howling in pain once more, Luke ran for the holding cave.

He reached the doorway and ran in. Before him, a heavy barred gate blocked the way. Beyond this gate, the Rancor's two keepers sat eating dinner. They looked up as Luke entered, then stood and walked toward the gate.

Luke turned around to see the monster coming angrily after him. He turned back to the gate and tried to open it. The keepers poked at him with their two-pronged spears, jabbed at him through the bars, laughing and chewing their food, as the Rancor drew closer to the young Jedi.

Luke backed against the side wall, as the Rancor reached in the room for him. Suddenly he saw the restraining-door control panel halfway up the opposite wall. The Rancor began to enter the holding room, closing for the kill, when all at once Luke picked up a skull off the floor and hurled it at the panel.

The panel exploded in a shower of sparks, and the giant iron overhead restraining door came crashing down on the Rancor's head, crushing it like an axe smashing through a ripe watermelon.

Those in the audience above gasped as one, then were silent. They were all truly stunned at this bizarre turn of events. They all looked to Jabba, who was apo-

plectic with rage. Never had he felt such fury. Leia
tried to hide her delight, but was unable to keep from
smiling, and this increased Jabba's anger even further.
Harshly he snapped at his guards: "Get him out of
there. Bring me Solo and the Wookiee. They will all
suffer for this outrage."

In the pit below, Luke stood calmly as several of
Jabba's henchmen ran in, clapped him in bonds, and
ushered him out.

The Rancor keeper wept openly and threw himself
down on the body of his dead pet. Life would be a
lonely proposition for him from that day.

Han and Chewie were led before the steaming Jabba.
Han still squinted and stumbled every few feet. Threepio stood behind the Hutt, unbearably apprehensive.
Jabba kept Leia on a short tether, stroking her hair to
try to calm himself. A constant murmuring filled the
room, as the rabble speculated on what was going to
happen to whom.

With a flurry, several guards—including Lando Calrissian—dragged Luke in across the room. To give them
passage, the courtiers parted like an unruly sea. When
Luke, too, was standing before the throne, he nudged
Solo with a smile. "Good to see you again, old buddy."

Solo's face lit up. There seemed to be no end to the
number of friends he kept bumping into. "Luke! Are
you in this mess now, too?"

"Wouldn't miss it," Skywalker smiled. For just a
moment, he almost felt like a boy again.

"Well, how we doing?" Han raised his eyebrows.

"Same as always," said Luke.

"Oh-oh," Solo replied under his breath. He felt one
hundred percent relaxed. Just like old times—but a
second later, a bleak thought chilled him.

"Where's Leia? Is she..."

Her eyes had been fixed on him from the moment
he'd entered the room, though—guarding his spirit
with her own. When he spoke of her now, she responded instantly, calling from her place on Jabba's

throne. "I'm all right, but I don't know how much longer I can hold off your slobbering friend, here." She was intentionally cavalier, to put Solo at ease. Besides, the sight of all of her friends there at once made her feel nearly invincible. Han, Luke, Chewie, Lando—even Threepio was skulking around somewhere, trying to be forgotten. Leia almost laughed out loud, almost punched Jabba in the nose. She could barely restrain herself. She wanted to hug them all.

Suddenly Jabba shouted; the entire room was immediately silent. "Talkdroid!"

Timidly, Threepio stepped forward and with an embarrassed, self-effacing head gesture, addressed the captives. "His High Exaltedness, the great Jabba the Hutt, has decreed that you are to be terminated immediately."

Solo said loudly, "That's good, I hate long waits..."

"Your extreme offense against His Majesty," Threepio went on, "demands the most torturous form of death..."

"No sense in doing things halfway," Solo cracked. Jabba could be so pompous, sometimes, and now with old Goldenrod, there, making his pronouncements...

No matter what else, Threepio simply *hated* being interrupted. He collected himself, nonetheless, and continued. "You will be taken to the Dune Sea, where you will be thrown into the Great Pit of Carkoon—"

Han shrugged, then turned to Luke. "That doesn't sound too bad."

Threepio ignored the interruption. "...the resting place of the all-powerful Sarlacc. In his belly you will find a new definition of pain and suffering, as you slowly digest for a thousand years."

"On second thought we could pass on that," Solo reconsidered. A thousand years was a bit much.

Chewie barked his whole-hearted agreement.

Luke only smiled. "You should have bargained, Jabba. This is the last mistake you'll ever make." Luke was unable to suppress the satisfaction in his voice. He found Jabba despicable—a leech of the galaxy, sucking the life from whatever he touched. Luke wanted to burn the villain, and so was actually rather glad Jabba had refused to bargain—for now Luke would get his wish precisely. Of course, his primary objective was to free his friends, whom he loved dearly; it was this concern that guided him now, above all else. But in the process, to free the universe of this gangster slug—this was a prospect that tinted Luke's purpose with an ever-so-slightly dark satisfaction.

Jabba chortled evilly. "Take them away." At last, a bit of pure pleasure on an otherwise dreary day—feeding the Sarlacc was the only thing he enjoyed as much as feeding the Rancor. Poor Rancor.

A loud cheer rose from the crowd as the prisoners were carried off. Leia looked after them with great concern; but when she caught a glimpse of Luke's face she was stirred to see it still fixed in a broad, genuine smile. She sighed deeply, to expel her doubts.

Jabba's giant antigravity Sail Barge glided slowly over the endless Dune Sea. Its sand-blasted iron hull creaked in the slight breeze, each puff of wind coughing into the two huge sails as if even nature suffered some terminal malaise wherever it came near Jabba. He was belowdecks, now, with most of his court, hiding the decay of his spirit from the cleansing sun.

Alongside the barge, two small skiffs floated in formation—one an escort craft, bearing six scruffy soldiers; the other, a gun skiff, containing the prisoners: Han, Chewie, Luke. They were all in bonds, and surrounded by armed guards—Barada, two Weequays. And Lando Calrissian.

Barada was the no-nonsense sort, and not likely to let anything get out of hand. He carried a long-gun as if he wanted nothing more than to hear it speak.

The Weequays were an odd sort. They were brothers, leathery and bald save for a tribal top-knot, braided and worn to the side. No one was certain whether Weequay was the name of their tribe, or their species; or whether all in their tribe were brothers, or all were named Weequays. It was known only that these two were called by this name, and that they treated all other creatures indifferently. With each other they were gentle, even tender; but like Barada, they seemed anxious for the prisoners to misbehave.

And Lando, of course, remained silent, ready—waiting for an opportunity. This reminded him of the lithium scam he'd run on Pesmenben IV—they'd salted the dunes there with lithium carbonate, to con this Imperial governor into leasing the planet. Lando, posing as a nonunion mine guard, had made the governor lie face down in the bottom of the boat and throw his bribe overboard when the "union officials" raided them. They'd gotten away scot-free on that one; Lando expected this job would go much the same, except they might have to throw the guards overboard as well.

Han kept his ear tuned, for his eyes were still useless. He spoke with reckless disregard, to put the guards at ease—to get them used to his talking and moving, so when the time came for him *really* to move, they'd be a critical fraction behind his mark. And, of course—as always—he spoke just to hear himself speak.

"I think my sight is getting better," he said, squinting over the sand. "Instead of a big dark blur, I see a big bright blur."

"Believe me, you're not missing anything." Luke smiled. "I grew up here."

Luke thought of his youth on Tatooine, living on his uncle's farm, cruising in his souped-up landspeeder with his few friends—sons of other settlers, sitting their own lonely outposts. Nothing ever to do here, really, for man or boy, but cruise the monotonous dunes and try to avoid the peevish Tusken Raiders who guarded the sand as if it were gold-dust. Luke knew this place.

He'd met Obi-Wan Kenobi, here—old Ben Kenobi, the hermit who'd lived in the wilderness since nobody knew when. The man who'd first shown Luke the way of the Jedi.

Luke thought of him now with great love, and great sorrow. For Ben was, more than anyone, the agent of

Luke's discoveries and losses—and discoveries *of* losses.

Ben had taken Luke to Mos Eisley, the pirate city on the western face of Tatooine, to the cantina where they'd first met Han Solo, and Chewbacca the Wookiee. Taken him there after Imperial stormtroopers had murdered Uncle Owen and Aunt Beru, searching for the fugitive droids, Artoo and Threepio.

That's how it had all started for Luke, here on Tatooine. Like a recurring dream he knew this place; and he had sworn then that he would never return.

"I grew up here," he repeated softly.

"And now we're going to die here," Solo replied.

"I wasn't planning on it," Luke shook himself out of his reverie.

"If this is your big plan, so far I'm not crazy about it."

"Jabba's palace was too well guarded. I had to get you out of there. Just stay close to Chewie and Lando. We'll take care of everything."

"I can hardly wait." Solo had a sinking feeling this grand escape depended on Luke's thinking he was a Jedi—a questionable premise at best, considering it was an extinct brotherhood that had used a Force he didn't really believe in anyway. A fast ship and a good blaster are what Han believed in, and he wished he had them now.

Jabba sat in the main cabin of the Sail Barge, surrounded by his entire retinue. The party at the palace was simply continuing, in motion—the result being a slightly wobblier brand of carousing—more in the nature of a prelynching celebration. So blood lust and belligerence were testing new levels.

Threepio was way out of his depth. At the moment, he was being forced to translate an argument between Ephant Mon and Ree-Yees, concerning a point of quark warfare that was marginally beyond him. Ephant Mon, a bulky upright pachydermoid with an ugly, betusked snout, was taking (to Threepio's way of thinking) an

untenable position. However, on his shoulder sat Salacious Crumb, the insane little reptilian monkey who
had the habit of repeating verbatim everything Ephant
said, thereby effectively doubling the weight of
Ephant's argument.

Ephant concluded the oration with a typically bel-
licose avowal. "Woossie jawamba boog!"

To which Salacious nodded, then added, "Woossie
jawamba boog!"

Threepio didn't really want to translate this to Ree-
Yees, the three-eyed goat-face who was already drunk
as a spicer, but he did.

All three eyes dilated in fury. "Backawa! Backawa!"
Without further preamble, he punched Ephant Mon in
the snout, sending him flying into a school of Squid
Heads.

See-Threepio felt this response needed no translation, and took the opportunity to slip to the rear—where
he promptly bumped into a small droid serving drinks.
The drinks spilled everywhere.

The stubby little droid let out a fluent series of irate
beeps, toots, and whistles—recognizable to Threepio
instantly. He looked down in utter relief. "Artoo! What
are you doing here?"

"doooWEEp chWHRrrrree bedzhng."

"I can see you're serving drinks. But this place is
dangerous. They're going to execute Master Luke, and
if we're not careful, us too!"

Artoo whistled—a bit nonchalantly, as far as Threepio was concerned. "I wish I had your confidence," he
replied glumly.

Jabba chuckled to see Ephant Mon go down—he
loved a good beating. He especially loved to see
strength crumble, to see the proud fall.

He tugged, with his swollen fingers, on the chain
attached to Princess Leia's neck. The more resistance
he met with, the more he drooled—until he'd drawn
the struggling, scantily-clad princess close to him once
more.

"Don't stray too far, my lovely. Soon you will begin

to appreciate me." He pulled her very near and forced her to drink from his glass.

Leia opened her mouth and she closed her mind. It was disgusting, of course; but there were worse things, and in any case, this wouldn't last.

The worse things she knew well. Her standard of comparison was the night she'd been tortured by Darth Vader. She had almost broken. The Dark Lord never knew how close he'd come to extracting the information he wanted from her, the location of the Rebel base. He had captured her just after she'd managed to send Artoo and Threepio for help—captured her, taken her to the Death Star, injected her with mind-weakening chemicals...and tortured her.

Tortured her body first, with his efficient pain-droids. Needles, pressure points, fire-knives, electrojabbers. She'd endured these pains, as she now endured Jabba's loathsome touch—with a natural, inner strength.

She slid a few feet away from Jabba, now, as his attention was distracted—moved to peer out the slats in the louvered windows, to squint through the dusty sunlight at the skiff on which her rescuers were being carried.

It was stopping.

The whole convoy was stopping, in fact, over a huge sand pit. The Sail Barge moved to one side of the giant depression, with the escort skiff. The prisoners' skiff hovered directly over the pit, though, perhaps twenty feet in the air.

At the bottom of the deep cone of sand, a repulsive, mucus-lined, pink, membranous hole puckered, almost unmoving. The hole was eight feet in diameter, its perimeter clustered with three rows of inwardly-directed needle-sharp teeth. Sand stuck to the mucus that lined the sides of the opening, occasionally sliding into the black cavity at the center.

This was the mouth of the Sarlacc.

An iron plank was extended over the side of the prisoners' skiff. Two guards untied Luke's bonds and shoved him gruffly out onto the plank, straight above the orifice in the sand, now beginning to undulate in peristaltic movement and salivate with increased mucus secretion as it smelled the meat it was about to receive.

Jabba moved his party up to the observation deck.

Luke rubbed his wrists to restore circulation. The heat shimmering off the desert warmed his soul—for finally, this would always be his home. Born and bred in a Bantha patch. He saw Leia standing at the rail of the big barge, and winked. She winked back.

Jabba motioned Threepio to his side, then mumbled orders to the golden droid. Threepio stepped up to the comlink. Jabba raised his arm, and the whole motley array of intergalactic pirates fell silent. Threepio's voice arose, amplified by the loudspeaker.

"His Excellency hopes you will die honorably," Threepio announced. This did not scan at all. Someone had obviously mislaid the correct program. Nonetheless, *he* was only a *droid*, his functions well delineated. Translation only, no free will *please*. He shook his head and continued. "But should any of you wish to beg for mercy, Jabba will now listen to your pleas."

Han stepped forward to give the bloated slime pot his last thoughts, in case all else failed. "You tell that slimy piece of worm-ridden filth—"

Unfortunately, Han was facing into the desert, away from the Sail Barge. Chewie reached over and turned Solo around, so he was now properly facing the piece of worm-ridden filth he was addressing.

Han nodded, without stopping. "—worm-ridden filth he'll get no such pleasure from us."

Chewie made a few growly noises of general agreement.

Luke was ready. "Jabba, this is your last chance," he shouted. "Free us or die." He shot a quick look to Lando, who moved unobtrusively toward the back of the skiff. This was it, Lando figured—they'd just toss the guards overboard and take off under everyone's nose.

The monsters on the barge roared with laughter.

Artoo, during this commotion, rolled silently up the ramp to the side of the upper deck.

Jabba raised his hand, and his minions were quiet. "I'm sure you're right, my young Jedi friend," he smiled. Then he turned his thumb down. "Put him in."

The spectators cheered, as Luke was prodded to the edge of the plank by Weequay. Luke looked up at Artoo, standing alone by the rail, and flipped the little droid a jaunty salute. At that prearranged signal, a flap slid open in Artoo's domed head, and a projectile shot high into the air and curved in a gentle arc over the desert.

Luke jumped off the plank; another bloodthirsty cheer went up. In less than a second, though, Luke had spun around in freefall, and caught the end of the plank with his fingertips. The thin metal bent wildly from his weight, paused near to snapping, then catapulted him up. In mid-air he did a complete flip and dropped down in the middle of the plank—the spot he'd just left, only now behind the confused guards. Casually, he extended his arm to his side, palm up— and suddenly, his lightsaber, which Artoo had shot sailing toward him, dropped neatly into his open hand.

With Jedi speed, Luke ignited his sword and attacked the guard at the skiff-edge of the plank, sending him, screaming, overboard into the twitching mouth of the Sarlacc.

The other guards swarmed toward Luke. Grimly he waded into them, lightsaber flashing.

His own lightsaber—not his father's. He had lost his father's in the duel with Darth Vader in which he'd lost his hand as well. Darth Vader, who had told Luke *he* was his father.

But this lightsaber Luke had fashioned himself, in Obi-Wan Kenobi's abandoned hut on the other side of Tatooine—made with the old Master Jedi's tools and parts, made with love and craft and dire need. He wielded it now as if it were fused to his hand; as if it were an extension of his own arm. This lightsaber, truly, was Luke's.

He cut through the onslaught like a light dissolving shadows.

Lando grappled with the helmsman, trying to seize the controls of the skiff. The helmsman's laser pistol fired, blasting the nearby panel; and the skiff lurched to the side, throwing another guard into the pit, knocking everyone else into a pile on the deck. Luke picked himself up and ran toward the helmsman, lightsaber raised. The creature retreated at the overpowering sight, stumbled...and he, too, went over the edge, into the maw.

The bewildered guard landed in the soft, sandy slope of the pit and began an inexorable slide down toward the toothy, viscous opening. He clawed desperately at the sand, screaming. Suddenly a muscled tentacle oozed out of the Sarlacc's mouth, slithered up the caked sand, coiled tightly around the helmsman's ankle, and pulled him into the hole with a grotesque slurp.

All this happened in a matter of seconds. When he saw what was happening, Jabba exploded in a rage, and yelled furious commands at those around him. In a moment, there was general uproar, with creatures running through every door. It was during this directionless confusion that Leia acted.

She jumped onto Jabba's throne, grabbed the chain which enslaved her, and wrapped it around his bulbous throat. Then she dove off the other side of the support, pulling the chain violently in her grasp. The small metal rings buried themselves in the loose folds of the Hutt's neck, like a garrote.

With a strength beyond her own strength, she pulled. He bucked with his huge torso, nearly breaking her fingers, nearly yanking her arms from their sockets. He could get no leverage, his bulk was too unwieldy. But just his sheer mass was almost enough to break any mere physical restraint.

Yet Leia's hold was not merely physical. She closed her eyes, closed out the pain in her hands, focused all of her life-force—and all it was able to channel—into squeezing the breath from the horrid creature.

She pulled, she sweated, she visualized the chain digging millimeter by millimeter deeper into Jabba's windpipe—as Jabba wildly thrashed, frantically twisted from this least expected of foes.

With a last gasping effort, Jabba tensed every muscle and lurched forward. His reptilian eyes began to bulge from their sockets as the chain tightened; his oily tongue flopped from his mouth. His thick tail twitched in spasms of effort, until he finally lay still—deadweight.

Leia set about trying to free herself from the chain at her neck, while outside, the battle began to rage.

Boba Fett ignited his rocket pack, leaped into the air, and with a single effort flew down from the barge to the skiff just as Luke finished freeing Han and Chewie from their bonds. Boba aimed his laser gun at Luke, but before he could fire, the young Jedi spun around, sweeping his lightsword in an arc that sliced the bounty hunter's gun in half.

A series of blasts suddenly erupted from the large cannon on the upper deck of the barge, hitting the skiff broadside, and rocking it forty degrees askew. Lando was tossed from the deck, but at the last moment he grabbed a broken strut and dangled desperately above the Sarlacc. This development was definitely not in his game plan, and he vowed to himself never again to get involved in a con that he didn't run from start to finish.

The skiff took another direct hit from the barge's deck gun, throwing Chewie and Han against the rail. Wounded, the Wookiee howled in pain. Luke looked over at his hairy friend; whereupon Boba Fett, taking advantage of that moment of distraction, fired a cable from out of his armored sleeve.

The cable wrapped itself several times around Luke, pinning his arms to his sides, his sword arm now free only from the wrist down. He bent his wrist, so the lightsaber pointed straight up...and then spun toward Boba along the cable. In a moment, the lightsaber touched the end of the wire lasso, cutting through it instantly. Luke shrugged the cable away, just as another blast hit the skiff, knocking Boba unconscious to the deck. Unfortunately this explosion also dislodged the strut from which Lando was hanging, sending him careening into the Sarlacc pit.

Luke was shaken by the explosion, but unhurt. Lando hit the sandy slope, shouted for help, and tried to scramble out. The loose sand only tumbled him deeper toward the gaping hole. Lando closed his eyes and tried to think of all the ways he might give the Sarlacc a thousand years of indigestion. He bet himself three to two he could outlast anybody else in the creature's stomach. Maybe if he talked that last guard out of his uniform...

"Don't move!" Luke screamed, but his attention was immediately diverted by the incoming second skiff, full of guards firing their weapons.

It was a Jedi rule-of-thumb, but it took the soldiers in the second skiff by surprise: when outnumbered, attack. This drives the force of the enemy in toward himself. Luke jumped directly into the center of the skiff and immediately began decimating them in their midst with lightning sweeps of his lightsaber.

Back in the other boat, Chewie tried to untangle himself from the wreckage, as Han struggled blindly to his feet. Chewie barked at him, trying to direct him toward a spear lying loose on the deck.

Lando screamed, starting to slide closer to the glistening jaws. He was a gambling man, but he wouldn't have taken long odds on his chances of escape right now.

"Don't move, Lando!" Han called out. "I'm coming!" Then, to Chewie: "Where is it, Chewie?" He swung his hands frantically over the deck as Chewie growled directions, guiding Solo's movements. At last, Han locked onto the spear.

Boba Fett stumbled up just then, still a little dizzy from the exploding shell. He looked over at the other skiff, where Luke was in a pitched battle with six guards. With one hand Boba steadied himself on the rail; with the other he aimed his weapon at Luke.

Chewie barked at Han.

"Which way?" shouted Solo. Chewie barked.

The blinded space pirate swung his long spear in Boba's direction. Instinctively, Fett blocked the blow with his forearm; again, he aimed at Luke. "Get out of my way, you blind fool," he cursed Solo.

Chewie barked frantically. Han swung his spear again, this time in the opposite direction, landing the hit squarely in the middle of Boba's rocket pack.

The impact caused the rocket to ignite. Boba blasted off unexpectedly, shooting over the second skiff like a missile and ricocheting straight down into the pit. His armored body slid quickly past Lando and rolled without pause into the Sarlacc's mouth.

"Rrgrrowrrbroo fro bo," Chewie growled.

"He did?" Solo smiled. "I wish I could have seen that—"

A major hit from the barge deck gun flipped the skiff on its side, sending Han and almost everything else overboard. His foot caught on the railing, though, leaving him swinging precariously above the Sarlacc. The wounded Wookiee tenaciously held on to the twisted debris astern.

Luke finished going through his adversaries on the second skiff, assessed the problem quickly, and leaped across the chasm of sand to the sheer metal side of the huge barge. Slowly, he began a hand-over-hand climb up the hull, toward the deck gun.

Meanwhile, on the observation deck, Leia had been intermittently struggling to break the chain which bound her to the dead gangster, and hiding behind his massive carcass whenever some guard ran by. She stretched her full length, now, trying to retrieve a discarded laser pistol—to no avail. Fortunately, Artoo at last came to her rescue, after having first lost his bearings and rolled down the wrong plank.

He zipped up to her finally, extended a cutting appendage from the side of his casing, and sliced through her bonds.

"Thanks, Artoo, good work. Now let's get out of here."

They raced for the door. On the way, they passed

Threepio, lying on the floor, screaming, as a giant, tuberous hulk named Hermi Odle sat on him. Salacious Crumb, the reptilian monkey-monster, crouched by Threepio's head, picking out the golden droid's right eye.

"No! No! Not my eyes!" Threepio screamed.

Artoo sent a bolt of charge into Hermi Odle's backside, sending him wailing through a window. A similar flash blasted Salacious to the ceiling, from which he didn't come down. Threepio quickly rose, his eye dangling from a sheaf of wires; then he and Artoo hurriedly followed Leia out the back door.

The deck gun blasted the tilting skiff once more, shaking out virtually everything that remained inside except Chewbacca. Desperately holding on with his injured arm, he was stretching over the rail, grasping the ankle of the dangling Solo, who was, in turn, sightlessly reaching down for the terrified Calrissian. Lando had managed to stop his slippage by lying very still. Now, every time he reached up for Solo's outstretched arm, the loose sand slid him a fraction closer to the hungry hole. He sure hoped Solo wasn't still holding that silly business back on Bespin against him.

Chewie barked another direction at Han.

"Yeah, I know, I can see a lot better now—it must be all the blood rushing to my head."

"Great," Lando called up. "Now could you just grow a few inches taller?"

The deck gunners on the barge were lining up this human chain in their sights for the coup de grace, when Luke stepped in front of them, laughing like a pirate king. He lit his lightsaber before they could squeeze off a shot; a moment later they were smoking corpses.

A company of guards suddenly rushed up the steps from the lower decks, firing. One of the blasts shot Luke's lightsaber from his hand. He ran down the deck, but was quickly surrounded. Two of the soldiers manned the deck gun again. Luke looked at his hand; the mechanism was exposed—the complex steel-and-

circuit construction that replaced his real hand, which
Vader had cut off in their last encounter.

He flexed the mechanism; it still worked.

The deck gunners fired at the skiff below. It hit to
the side of the small boat. The shock wave almost
knocked Chewie loose, but in tipping the boat further,
Han was able to grab onto Lando's wrist.

"Pull!" Solo yelled at the Wookiee.

"I'm caught!" screamed Calrissian. He looked down
in panic to see one of the Sarlacc's tentacles slowly
wrap around his ankle. Talk about a wild card—they
kept changing the rules every five minutes in this game.
Tentacles! What kind of odds was anybody gonna give
on tentacles? Very long, he decided with a fatalistic
grunt; long, and sticky.

The deck gunners realigned their sights for the final
kill, but it was all over for them before they could fire—
Leia had commandeered the second deck gun, at the
other end of the ship. With her first shot she blasted
the rigging that stood between the two deck guns. With
her second shot she wiped out the first deck gun.

The explosions rocked the great barge, momentarily
distracting the five guards who surrounded Luke. In
that moment he reached out his hand, and the lightsaber, lying on the deck ten feet away, flew into it. He
leaped straight up as two guards fired at him—their
laser bolts killed each other. He ignited his blade in
the air and, swinging it as he came down, mortally
wounded the others.

He yelled to Leia across the deck. "Point it down!"

She tilted the second deck gun into the deck and
nodded to Threepio at the rail.

Artoo, beside him, beeped wildly.

"I can't, Artoo!" Threepio cried. "It's too far to
jump…aaahhh!"

Artoo butted the golden droid over the edge, and
then stepped off himself, tumbling head over wheels
toward the sand.

Meanwhile, the tug-of-war was continuing between

the Sarlacc and Solo, with Baron Calrissian as the rope
and the prize. Chewbacca held Han's leg, braced himself on the rail, and succeeded in pulling a laser pistol
out of the wreckage with his other hand. He aimed the
gun toward Lando, then lowered it, barking his concern.

"He's right!" Lando called out. "It's too far!"

Solo looked up. "Chewie, give me the gun."

Chewbacca gave it to him. He took it with one hand,
still holding on to Lando with the other.

"Now, wait a second, pal," Lando protested, "I
thought you were blind."

"I'm better, trust me," Solo assured him.

"Do I have a choice? Hey! A little higher, please."
He lowered his head.

Han squinted...pulled the trigger...and scored a
direct hit on the tentacle. The wormy thing instantly
released its grip, slithering back into its own mouth.

Chewbacca pulled mightily, drawing first Solo back
into the boat—and then Lando.

Luke, meantime, gathered Leia up in his left arm;
with his right he grabbed a hold of a rope from the
rigging of the half blown-down mast, and with his foot
kicked the trigger of the second deck gun—and jumped
into the air as the cannon exploded into the deck.

The two of them swung on the swaying rope, all the
way down to the empty, hovering escort skiff. Once
there, Luke steered it over to the still-listing prison
skiff, where he helped Chewbacca, Han, and Lando
on board.

The Sail Barge continued exploding behind them.
Half of it was now on fire.

Luke guided the skiff around beside the barge, where
See-Threepio's legs could be seen sticking straight up
out of the sand. Beside them, Artoo-Detoo's periscope
was the only part of his anatomy visible above the
dune. The skiff stopped just above them and lowered
a large electromagnet from its compartment in the boat's
helm. With a loud clang, the two droids shot out of the
sand and locked to the magnet's plate.

"Ow," groaned Threepio.

"beeeDOO dwEET!" Artoo agreed.

In a few minutes, they were all in the skiff together, more or less in one piece; and for the first time, they looked at one another and realized they were all in the skiff together, more or less in one piece. There was a great, long moment of hugging, laughing, crying, and beeping. Then someone accidentally squeezed Chewbacca's wounded arm, and he bellowed; and then they all ran about, securing the boat, checking the perimeters, looking for supplies—and sailing away.

The great Sail Barge settled slowly in a chain of explosions and violent fires, and—as the little skiff flew quietly off across the desert—disappeared finally in a brilliant conflagration that was only partially diminished by the scorching afternoon light of Tatooine's twin suns.

3

THE sandstorm obscured everything—sight, breath, thought, motion. The roar of it alone was disorienting, sounding like it came from everywhere at once, as if the universe were composed of noise, and this was its chaotic center.

The seven heroes walked step by step through the murky gale, holding on to one another so as not to get lost. Artoo was first, following the signal of the homing device which sang to him in a language not garbled by the wind. Threepio came next, then Leia guiding Han, and finally Luke and Lando, supporting the hobbling Wookiee.

Artoo beeped loudly, and they all looked up: vague, dark shapes could be seen through the typhoon.

"I don't know," shouted Han. "All I can see is a lot of blowing sand."

"That's all any of us can see," Leia shouted back.

"Then I guess I'm getting better."

For a few steps, the dark shapes grew darker; and then out of the darkness, the *Millennium Falcon* appeared, flanked by Luke's X-wing and a two-seater Y-wing. As soon as the group huddled under the bulk of the *Falcon*, the wind died down to something more describable as a severe weather condition. Threepio hit a switch, and the gangplank lowered with a hum.

Solo turned to Skywalker. "I've got to hand it to you, kid, you were pretty good out there."

Luke shrugged it off. "I had a lot of help." He started toward his X-wing.

Han stopped him, his manner suddenly quieter, even serious. "Thanks for coming after me, Luke."

Luke felt embarrassed for some reason. He didn't know how to respond to anything but a wisecrack from the old pirate. "Think nothing of it," he finally said.

"No, I'm thinkin' a lot about it. That carbon freeze was the closest thing to dead there is. And it wasn't just sleepin', it was a big, wide awake Nothin'."

A Nothing from which Luke and the others had saved him—put their own lives in great peril at his expense, for no other reason than that...he was their friend. This was a new idea for the cocky Solo—at once terrible and wonderful. There was jeopardy in this turn of events. It made him feel somehow blinder than before, but visionary as well. It was confusing. Once, he was alone; now he was a part.

That realization made him feel indebted, a feeling he'd always abhorred; only now the debt was somehow a new kind of bond, a bond of brotherhood. It was even freeing, in a strange way.

He was no longer so alone.

No longer alone.

Luke saw a difference had come over his friend, like a sea change. It was a gentle moment; he didn't want to disturb it. So he only nodded.

Chewie growled affectionately at the young Jedi warrior, mussing his hair like a proud uncle. And Leia warmly hugged him.

They all had great love for Solo, but somehow it was easier to show it by being demonstrative to Luke.

"I'll see you back at the fleet," Luke called, moving toward his ship.

"Why don't you leave that crate and come with us?" Solo nudged.

"I have a promise I have to keep first...to an old friend." A *very* old friend, he smiled to himself in afterthought.

"Well, hurry back," Leia urged. "The entire Alliance should be assembled by now." She saw something in Luke's face; she couldn't put a name to it, but it scared her, and simultaneously made her feel closer to him. "Hurry back," she repeated.

"I will," he promised. "Come on, Artoo."

Artoo rolled toward the X-wing, beeping a farewell to Threepio.

"Good-bye, Artoo," Threepio called out fondly. "May the maker bless you. You will watch out for him, won't you, Master Luke?"

But Luke and the little droid were already gone, on the far side of the flyer.

The others stood without moving for a moment, trying to see their futures in the swirling sand.

Lando jarred them awake. "Come on, let's get off this miserable dirt ball." His luck here had been abominable; he hoped to fare better in the next game. It would be house rules for a while, he knew; but he might be able to load a few dice along the way.

Solo clapped him on the back. "Guess I owe you some thanks, too, Lando."

"Figured if I left you frozen like that you'd just give me bad luck the rest of my life, so I might as well get you unfrozen sooner, as later."

"He means 'you're welcome.'" Leia smiled. "We all mean you're welcome." She kissed Han on the cheek to say it personally one more time.

They all headed up the ramp of the *Falcon*. Solo paused just before going inside and gave the ship a little pat. "You're lookin' good, old girl. I never thought I'd live to see you again."

He entered at last, closing the hatch behind him.

Luke did the same in the X-wing. He strapped himself into the cockpit, started up the engines, felt the comfortable roar. He looked at his damaged hand: wires crossed aluminum bones like spokes in a puzzle. He wondered what the solution was. Or the puzzle, for that matter. He pulled a black glove over the exposed infrastructure, set the X-wing's controls, and for the second time in his life, he rocketed off his home planet, into the stars.

The Super Star Destroyer rested in space above the half-completed Death Star battle station and its green neighbor, Endor. The Destroyer was a massive ship, attended by numerous smaller warships of various kinds, which hovered or darted around the great mother ship like children of different ages and temperaments: medium range fleet cruisers, bulky cargo vessels, TIE fighter escorts.

The main bay of the Destroyer opened, space-silent. An Imperial shuttle emerged and accelerated toward the Death Star, accompanied by four squads of fighters.

Darth Vader watched their approach on the viewscreen in the control room of the Death Star. When docking was imminent, he marched out of the command center, followed by Commander Jerjerrod and a phalanx of Imperial stormtroopers, and headed toward the docking bay. He was about to welcome his master.

Vader's pulse and breathing were machine-regulated, so they could not quicken; but something in his chest became more electric around his meetings with the Emperor; he could not say how. A feeling of fullness, of power, of dark and demon mastery—of secret lusts, unrestrained passion, wild submission—all these things were in Vader's heart as he neared his Emperor. These things and more.

When he entered the docking bay, thousands of Imperial troops snapped to attention with a momentous clap. The shuttle came to rest on the pod. Its ramp lowered like a dragon jaw, and the Emperor's royal guard ran down, red robes flapping, as if they were licks of flame shooting out the mouth to herald the angry roar. They poised themselves at watchful guard in two lethal rows beside the ramp. Silence filled the great hall. At the top of the ramp, the Emperor appeared.

Slowly, he walked down. A small man was he, shriveled with age and evil. He supported his bent frame on a gnarled cane and covered himself with a long, hooded robe—much like the robe of the Jedi, only black. His shrouded face was so thin of flesh it was nearly a skull; his piercing yellow eyes seemed to burn through all at which they stared.

When the Emperor reached the bottom of the ramp, Commander Jerjerrod, his generals, and Lord Vader all kneeled before him. The Supreme Dark Ruler beckoned to Vader, and began walking down the row of troops.

"Rise, my friend. I would talk with you."

Vader rose, and accompanied his master. They were followed in procession by the Emperor's courtiers, the royal guard, Jerjerrod, and the Death Star elite guard, with mixed reverence and fear.

Vader felt complete at the Emperor's side. Though the emptiness at his core never left him, it became a glorious emptiness in the glare of the Emperor's cold light, an exalted void that could encompass the universe. And someday *would* encompass the universe ...when the Emperor was dead.

For that was Vader's final dream. When he'd learned all he could of the dark power from this evil genius, to take that power from him, seize it and keep its cold light at his own core—kill the Emperor and devour his darkness, and rule the universe. Rule with his son at his side.

For that was his other dream—to reclaim his boy, to show Luke the majesty of this shadow force: why it was so potent, why he'd chosen rightly to follow its path. And Luke would come with him, he knew. That seed was sown. They would rule together, father and son.

His dream was very close to realization, he could feel it; it was near. Each event fell into place, as he'd nudged it, with Jedi subtlety; as he'd pressed, with delicate dark strength.

"The Death Star will be completed on schedule, my master," Vader breathed.

"Yes, I know," replied the Emperor. "You have done well, Lord Vader...and now I sense you wish to continue your search for the young Skywalker."

Vader smiled beneath his armored mask. The Emperor always knew the sense of what was in his heart; even if he didn't know the specifics. "Yes, my master."

"Patience, my friend," the Supreme Ruler cautioned. "You always had difficulty showing patience. In time, *he* will seek *you* out...and when he does, you must bring him before me. He has grown strong. Only together can we turn him to the dark side of the Force."

"Yes, my master." Together, they would corrupt the boy—the child of the father. Great, dark glory. For soon, the old Emperor would die—and though the galaxy would bend from the horror of that loss, Vader would remain to rule, with young Skywalker at his side. As it was always meant to be.

The Emperor raised his head a degree, scanning all the possible futures. "Everything is proceeding as I have foreseen."

He, like Vader, had plans of his own—plans of spiritual violation, the manipulation of lives and destinies. He chuckled to himself, savoring the nearness of his conquest: the final seduction of the young Skywalker.

Luke left his X-wing parked at the edge of the water and carefully picked his way through the adjoining swamp. A heavy mist hung in layers about him. Jungle steam. A strange insect flew at him from out of a cluster of hanging vines, fluttered madly about his head, and vanished. In the undergrowth, something snarled. Luke concentrated momentarily. The snarling stopped. Luke walked on.

He had terribly ambivalent feelings about this place.

Dagobah. His place of tests, of training to be a Jedi. This was where he'd truly learned to use the Force, to let it flow through him to whatever end he directed it. So he'd learned how caretaking he must be in order to use the Force well. It was walking on light; but to a Jedi it was as stable as an earthen floor.

Dangerous creatures lurked in this swamp; but to a Jedi, none were evil. Voracious quicksand mires waited, still as pools; tentacles mingled with the hanging vines. Luke knew them all, now, they were all part of the living planet, each integral to the Force of which he, too, was a pulsing aspect.

Yet there were dark things here, as well—unimaginably dark, reflections of the dark corners of his soul. He'd seen these things here. He'd run from them, he'd struggled with them; he'd even faced them. He'd vanquished some of them.

But some still cowered here. These dark things.

He climbed around a barricade of gnarled roots, slippery with moss. On the other side, a smooth, unimpeded path led straight in the direction he wanted to go; but he did not take it. Instead, he plunged once more into the undergrowth.

High overhead, something black and flapping approached, then veered away. Luke paid no attention. He just kept walking.

The jungle thinned a bit. Beyond the next bog, Luke saw it—the small, strangely-shaped dwelling, its odd little windows shedding a warm yellow light in the damp rain-forest. He skirted the mire, and crouching low, entered the cottage.

Yoda stood smiling inside, his small green hand clutching his walking stick for support. "Waiting for you I was," he nodded.

He motioned Luke to sit in a corner. The boy was struck by how much more frail Yoda's manner seemed— a tremor to the hand, a weakness to the voice. It made Luke afraid to speak, to betray his shock at the old master's condition.

"That face you make," Yoda crinkled his tired brow cheerfully. "Look I so bad to young eyes?"

He tried to conceal his woeful countenance, shifting his position in the cramped space. "No, Master...of course not."

"I do, yes, I do!" the tiny Jedi Master chuckled gleefully. "Sick I've become. Yes. Old and weak." He pointed a crooked finger at his young pupil. "When nine hundred years old you reach, look as good you will not."

The creature hobbled over to his bed, still chuckling and, with great effort, lay down. "Soon will I rest. Yes, forever sleep. Earned it, I have."

Luke shook his head. "You can't die, Master Yoda— I won't let you."

"Trained well, and strong with the Force are you— but not that strong! Twilight is upon me, and soon night must fall. That is the way of things...the way of the Force."

"But I need your help," Luke insisted. "I want to complete my training." The great teacher couldn't leave him now—there was too much, still, to understand. And he'd taken so much from Yoda already, and as yet given back nothing. He had much he wanted to share with the old creature.

"No more training do you require," Yoda assured him. "Already know you that which you need."

"Then I am a Jedi?" Luke pressed. No. He knew he was not, quite. Something still lacked.

Yoda wrinkled up his wizened features. "Not yet. One thing remains. Vader...Vader you must confront. Then, only then, a full Jedi you'll be. And confront him you will, sooner or later."

Luke knew this would be his test, it could not be otherwise. Every quest had its focus, and Vader was inextricably at the core of Luke's struggle. It was agonizing for him to put the question to words; but after a long silence, he again spoke to the old Jedi. "Master Yoda—is Darth Vader my father?"

Yoda's eyes filled with a weary compassion. This boy was not yet a man complete. A sad smile creased his face, he seemed almost to grow smaller in his bed. "A rest I need. Yes. A rest."

Luke stared at the dwindling teacher, trying to give the old one strength, just by the force of his love and will. "Yoda, I must know," he whispered.

"Your father he is," Yoda said simply.

Luke closed his eyes, his mouth, his heart, to keep away the truth of what he knew was true.

"Told you, did he?" Yoda asked.

Luke nodded, but did not speak. He wanted to keep the moment frozen, to shelter it here, to lock time and space in this room, so it could never escape into the rest of the universe with this terrible knowledge, this unrelenting truth.

A look of concern filled Yoda's face. "Unexpected this is, and unfortunate—"

"Unfortunate that I know the truth?" A bitterness crept into Luke's voice, but he couldn't decide if it was directed at Vader, Yoda, himself, or the universe at large.

Yoda gathered himself up with an effort that seemed to take all his strength. "Unfortunate that you rushed to face him—that incomplete your training was...that not ready for the burden were you. Obi-Wan would have told you long ago, had I let him...now a great weakness you carry. Fear for you, I do. Fear for you, yes." A great tension seemed to pass out of him and he closed his eyes.

"Master Yoda, I'm sorry." Luke trembled to see the potent Jedi so weak.

"I know, but face Vader again you must, and sorry will not help." He leaned forward, and beckoned Luke close to him. Luke crawled over to sit beside his master. Yoda continued, his voice increasingly frail. "Remember, a Jedi's strength flows from the Force. When you rescued your friends, you had revenge in your heart. Beware of anger, fear, and aggression. The dark side are they. Easily they flow, quick to join you in a fight. Once you start down the dark path, forever will it dominate your destiny."

He lay back in bed, his breathing became shallow. Luke waited quietly, afraid to move, afraid to distract the old one an iota, lest it jar his attention even a fraction from the business of just keeping the void at bay.

After a few minutes, Yoda looked at the boy once more, and with a maximum effort, smiled gently, the greatness of his spirit the only thing keeping his decrepit body alive. "Luke—of the Emperor beware. Do not underestimate his powers, or suffer your father's fate you will. When gone I am...last of the Jedi will you be. Luke, the Force is strong in your family. Pass on what you...have...learned..." He began to falter, he closed his eyes. "There...is...another...sky..."

He caught his breath, and exhaled, his spirit passing from him like a sunny wind blowing to another sky. His body shivered once; and he disappeared.

Luke sat beside the small, empty bed for over an hour, trying to fathom the depth of this loss. It was unfathomable.

His first feeling was one of boundless grief. For himself, for the universe. How could such a one as Yoda be gone forever? It felt like a black, bottomless hole had filled his heart, where the part that was Yoda had lived.

Luke had known the passing of old mentors before. It was helplessly sad; and inexorably, a part of his own growing. Is this what coming of age was, then? Watching beloved friends grow old and die? Gaining a new measure of strength or maturity from their powerful passages?

A great weight of hopelessness settled upon him, just as all the lights in the little cottage flickered out. For several more minutes he sat there, feeling it was the end of everything, that all the lights in the universe had flickered out. The last Jedi, sitting in a swamp, while the entire galaxy plotted the last war.

A chill came over him, though, disturbing the nothingness into which his consciousness had lapsed. He shivered, looked around. The gloom was impenetrable.

He crawled outside and stood up. Here in the swamp, nothing had changed. Vapor congealed, to drip from dangling roots back into the mire, in a cycle it had repeated a million times, would repeat forever. Perhaps *there* was his lesson. If so, it cut his sadness not a whit.

Aimlessly he made his way back to where his ship rested. Artoo rushed up, beeping his excited greeting; but Luke was disconsolate, and could only ignore the faithful little droid. Artoo whistled a brief condolence, then remained respectfully silent.

Luke sat dejectedly on a log, put his head in his hands, and spoke softly to himself. "I can't do it. I can't go on alone."

A voice floated down to him on the dim mist. "Yoda and I will be with you always." It was Ben's voice.

Luke turned around swiftly to see the shimmering image of Obi-Wan Kenobi standing behind him. "Ben!" he whispered. There were so many things he wanted to say, they rushed through his mind all in a whirl, like the churning, puffed cargo of a ship in a maelstrom. But one question rose quickly to the surface above all the others. "Why, Ben? Why didn't you tell me?"

It was not an empty question. "I was going to tell you when you had completed your training," the vision of Ben answered. "But you found it necessary to rush off unprepared. I warned you about your impatience." His voice was unchanged, a hint of scolding, a hint of love.

"You told me Darth Vader betrayed and murdered my father." The bitterness he'd felt earlier, with Yoda, had found its focus now on Ben.

Ben absorbed the vitriol undefensively, then padded it with instruction. "Your father, Anakin, was seduced by the dark side of the Force—He ceased to be Anakin Skywalker, and became Darth Vader. When that happened, he betrayed everything that Anakin

Skywalker believed in. The good man who was your father was destroyed. So what I told you was true...from a certain point of view."

"A certain point of view!" Luke rasped derisively. He felt betrayed—by life more than anything else, though only poor Ben was available to take the brunt of his conflict.

"Luke," Ben spoke gently, "you're going to find that many of the truths we cling to depend greatly on our point of view."

Luke turned unresponsive. He wanted to hold onto his fury, to guard it like a treasure. It was all he had, he would not let it be stolen from him, as everything else had been stolen. But already he felt it slipping, softened by Ben's compassionate touch.

"I don't blame you for being angry," Ben coaxed. "If I was wrong in what I did, it certainly wouldn't have been for the first time. You see, what happened to your father was my fault..."

Luke looked up with sudden acute interest. He'd never heard this and was rapidly losing his anger to fascination and curiosity—for knowledge was an addictive drug, and the more he had the more he wanted.

As he sat on his stump, increasingly mesmerized, Artoo pedaled over, silent, just to offer a comforting presence.

"When I first encountered your father," Ben continued, "he was already a great pilot. But what amazed me was how strongly the Force was with him. I took it upon myself to train Anakin in the ways of the Jedi. My mistake was thinking I could be as good a teacher as Yoda. I was not. Such was my foolish pride. The Emperor sensed Anakin's power, and he lured him to the dark side." He paused sadly and looked directly into Luke's eyes, as if he were asking for the boy's forgiveness. "My pride had terrible consequences for the galaxy."

Luke was entranced. That Obi-Wan's hubris could have caused his father's fall was horrible. Horrible because of what his father had needlessly become, horrible because Obi-Wan wasn't perfect, wasn't even a perfect Jedi, horrible because the dark side could strike so close to home, could turn such right so wrong. Darth Vader must yet have a spark of Anakin Skywalker deep inside. "There is still good in him," he declared.

Ben shook his head remorsefully. "I also thought he could be turned back to the good side. It couldn't be done. He is more machine, now, than man—twisted, and evil."

Luke sensed the underlying meaning in Kenobi's statement, he heard the words as a command. He shook his head back at the vision. "I can't kill my own father."

"You should not think of that machine as your father." It was the teacher speaking again. "When I saw what had become of him, I tried to dissuade him, to draw him back from the dark side. We fought...your father fell into a molten pit. When your father clawed his way out of that fiery pool, the change had been burned into him forever—he was Darth Vader, without a trace of Anakin Skywalker. Irredeemably dark. Scarred. Kept alive only by machinery and his own black will..."

Luke looked down at his own mechanical right hand. "I tried to stop him once. I couldn't do it." He would not challenge his father again. He could not.

"Vader humbled you when first you met him, Luke— but that experience was *part* of your training. It taught you, among other things, the value of patience. Had you not been so impatient to defeat Vader *then*, you could have finished your training here with Yoda. You would have been prepared."

"But I had to help my friends."

"And did you help them? It was *they* who had to save *you*. You achieved little by rushing back prematurely, I fear."

Luke's indignation melted, leaving only sadness in its wake. "I found out Darth Vader was my father," he whispered.

"To be a Jedi, Luke, you must confront and then go beyond the dark side—the side your father couldn't get past. Impatience is the easiest door—for you, like your father. Only, your father was seduced by what he found on the other side of the door, and you have held firm. You're no longer so reckless now, Luke. You are strong and patient. And you are ready for your final confrontation."

Luke shook his head again, as the implications of the old Jedi's speech became clear. "I can't do it, Ben."

Obi-Wan Kenobi's shoulders slumped in defeat. "Then the Emperor has already won. You were our only hope."

Luke reached for alternatives. "Yoda said I could train another to..."

"The other he spoke of is your twin sister," the old man offered a dry smile. "She will find it no easier than you to destroy Darth Vader."

Luke was visibly jolted by this information. He stood up to face this spirit. "Sister? I don't have a sister."

Once again Obi-Wan put a gentle inflection in his voice, to soothe the turmoil brewing in his young friend's soul. "To protect you both against the Emperor, you were separated when you were born. The Emperor knew, as I did, that one day, with the Force on their side, Skywalker's offspring would be a threat to him. For that reason, your sister has remained safely anonymous."

Luke resisted this knowledge at first. He neither needed nor wanted a twin. He was unique! He had no missing parts—save the hand whose mechanical replacement he now flexed tightly. Pawn in a castle conspiracy? Cribs mixed, siblings switched and parted and whisked away to different secret lives? Impossible. He knew who he was! He was Luke Skywalker, born to a Jedi-turned-Sithlord, raised on a Tatooine sandfarm by Uncle Owen and Aunt Beru, raised in a life without frills, a hardworking honest pauper—because his mother...his mother...What was it about his mother? What had she said, who was she? What had she told him? He turned his mind inward, to a place and time far from the damp soil of Dagobah, to his mother's chamber, his mother and his...sister. His sister...

"Leia! Leia is my sister," he exclaimed, nearly falling over the stump.

"Your insight serves you well," Ben nodded. He quickly became stern, though. "Bury your feelings deep down, Luke. They do you credit, but they could be made to serve the Emperor."

Luke tried to comprehend what his old teacher was saying. So much information, so fast, so vital...it almost made him swoon.

Ben continued his narrative. "When your father left, he didn't know your mother was pregnant. Your mother and I knew he would find out eventually, but we wanted to keep you both as safe as possible, for as long as possible. So I took you to live with my brother Owen, on Tatooine...and your mother took Leia to live as the daughter of Senator Organa, on Alderaan."

Luke settled down to hear this tale, as Artoo nestled up beside him, humming in a subaudible register to comfort.

Ben, too, kept his voice even, so that the sounds could give solace when the words did not. "The Organa family was high-born and politically quite powerful in that system. Leia became a princess by virtue of lineage—no one knew she'd been adopted, of course. But it was a title without real power, since Alderaan had long been a democracy. Even so, the family continued to be politically powerful, and Leia, following in her foster father's path, became a senator as well. That's not all she became, of course—she became the leader of her cell in the Alliance against the corrupt Empire. And because she had diplomatic immunity, she was a vital link for getting information to the Rebel cause.

"That's what she was doing when her path crossed yours—for her foster parents had always told her to contact *me* on Tatooine, if her troubles became desperate."

Luke tried sorting through his multiplicity of feelings—the love he'd always felt for Leia, even from afar, now had a clear basis. But suddenly he was feeling protective toward her as well, like an older brother—

even though, for all he knew, she might have been his elder by several minutes.

"But you can't let her get involved now, Ben," he insisted. "Vader will destroy her." Vader. Their father. Perhaps Leia *could* resurrect the good in him.

"She hasn't been trained in the ways of the Jedi the way you have, Luke—but the Force is strong with her, as it is with all of your family. That is why her path crossed mine—because the Force in her must be nourished by a Jedi. You're the last Jedi, now, Luke...but she returned to us—to me—to learn, and grow. Because it was her destiny to learn and grow; and mine to teach."

He went on more slowly, each word deliberate, each pause emphatic. "You cannot escape your destiny, Luke." He locked his eyes on Luke's eyes, and put as much of his spirit as he could into the gaze, to leave it forever imprinted on Luke's mind. "Keep your sister's identity secret, for if you fail she is truly our last hope. Gaze on me now, Luke—the coming fight is yours alone, but much will depend on its outcome, and it may be that you can draw some strength from my memory. There is no avoiding the battle, though—you can't escape your destiny. You will have to face Darth Vader again..."

☐ 4

DARTH Vader stepped out of the long, cylindrical elevator into what had been the Death Star control room, and now was the Emperor's throne room. Two royal guards stood either side of the door, red robes from neck to toe, red helmets covering all but eyeslits that were actually electrically modified view-screens. Their weapons were always drawn.

The room was dim except for the light cables running either side of the elevator shaft, carrying power and information through the space station. Vader walked across the sleek black steel floor, past the humming giant converter engines, up the short flight of steps to the platform level upon which sat the Emperor's throne. Beneath this platform, off to the right, was the mouth of the shaft that delved deeply into the pit of the battle station, down to the very core of the power unit. The chasm was black, and reeked of ozone, and echoed continuously in a low, hollow rumble.

At the end of the overhanging platform was a wall, in the wall, a huge, circular observation window. Sitting in an elaborate control-chair before the window, staring out into space, was the Emperor.

The uncompleted half of the Death Star could be seen immediately beyond the window, shuttles and transports buzzing around it, men with tight-suits and rocket-packs doing exterior construction or surface work. In the near-distance beyond all this activity was the jade green moon Endor, resting like a jewel on the black velvet of space—and scattered to infinity, the gleaming diamonds that were the stars.

The Emperor sat, regarding this view, as Vader approached from behind. The Lord of the Sith kneeled and waited. The Emperor let him wait. He perused the vista before him with a sense of glory beyond all reckoning: this was all his. And more glorious still, all his by his own hand.

For it wasn't always so. Back in the days when he was merely Senator Palpatine, the galaxy had been a Republic of stars, cared for and protected by the Jedi Knighthood that had watched over it for centuries. But inevitably it had grown too large—too massive a bureaucracy had been required, over too many years, in order to maintain the Republic. Corruption had set in.

A few greedy senators had started the chain reaction of malaise, some said; but who could know? A few perverted bureaucrats, arrogant, self-serving—and suddenly a fever was in the stars. Governor turned on governor, values eroded, trusts were broken—fear had spread like an epidemic in those early years, rapidly and without visible cause, and no one knew what was happening, or why.

And so Senator Palpatine had seized the moment. Through fraud, clever promises, and astute political maneuvering, he'd managed to get himself elected head of the Council. And then through subterfuge, bribery and terror, he'd named himself Emperor.

Emperor. It had a certain ring to it. The Republic had crumbled, the Empire was resplendent with its own fires, and would always be so—for the Emperor

knew what others refused to believe: the dark forces
were the strongest.

He'd known this all along, in his heart of hearts—
but relearned it every day: from traitorous lieutenants
who betrayed their superiors for favors; from weak-
principled functionaries who gave him the secrets of
local star systems' governments; from greedy land-
lords, and sadistic gangsters, and power-hungry poli-
ticians. No one was immune, they all craved the dark
energy at their core. The Emperor had simply recog-
nized this truth, and utilized it—for his own aggran-
dizement, of course.

For his soul was the black center of the Empire.

He contemplated the dense impenetrability of the
deep space beyond the window. Densely black as his
soul—as if he *were*, in some real way, this blackness;
as if his inner spirit was itself this void over which he
reigned. He smiled at the thought: he *was* the Empire;
he *was* the Universe.

Behind him, he sensed Vader still waiting in genu-
flection. How long had the Dark Lord been there?
Five minutes? Ten? The Emperor was uncertain. No
matter. The Emperor had not quite finished his med-
itation.

Lord Vader did not mind waiting, though, nor was
he even aware of it. For it was an honor, and a noble
activity, to kneel at his ruler's feet. He kept his eyes
inward, seeking reflection in his own bottomless core.
His power was great, now, greater than it had ever
been. It shimmered from within, and resonated with
the waves of darkness that flowed from the Emperor.
He felt engorged with this power, it surged like black
fire, demon electrons looking for ground...but he would
wait. For his Emperor was not ready; and his son was
not ready, and the time was not yet. So he waited.

Finally the chair slowly rotated until the Emperor
faced Vader.

Vader spoke first. "What is thy bidding, my master?"

"Send the fleet to the far side of Endor. There it
will stay until called for."

"And what of the reports of the Rebel fleet massing near Sullust?"

"It is of no concern. Soon the Rebellion will be crushed and young Skywalker will be one of us. Your work here is finished, my friend. Go out to the command ship and await my orders."

"Yes, my master." He hoped he would be given command over the destruction of the Rebel Alliance. He hoped it would be soon.

He rose and exited, as the Emperor turned back to the galactic panorama beyond the window, to view his domain.

In a remote and midnight vacuum beyond the edge of the galaxy, the vast Rebel fleet stretched, from its vanguard to its rear echelon, past the range of human vision. Corellian battle ships, cruisers, destroyers, carriers, bombers, Sullustian cargo freighters, Calamarian tankers, Alderaanian gunships, Kesselian blockade runners, Bestinian skyhoppers, X-wing, Y-wing, and A-wing fighters, shuttles, transport vehicles, manowars. Every Rebel in the galaxy, soldier and civilian alike, waited tensely in these ships for instructions. They were led by the largest of the Rebel Star Cruisers, the *Headquarters Frigate.*

Hundreds of Rebel commanders, of all species and lifeforms, assembled in the war room of the giant Star Cruiser, awaiting orders from the High Command. Rumors were everywhere, and an air of excitement spread from squadron to squadron.

At the center of the briefing room was a large, circular light-table, projected above which a holographic image of the unfinished Imperial Death Star hovered beside the Moon of Endor, whose scintillating protective deflector shield encompassed them both.

Mon Mothma entered the room. A stately, beautiful woman of middle age, she seemed to walk above the murmurs of the crowd. She wore white robes with gold braiding, and her severity was not without cause—for she was the elected leader of the Rebel Alliance.

Like Leia's adopted father—like Palpatine the Emperor himself—Mon Mothma had been a senior senator of the Republic, a member of the High Council. When the Republic had begun to crumble, Mon Mothma had remained a senator until the end, organizing dissent, stabilizing the increasingly ineffectual government.

She had organized cells, too, toward the end. Pockets of resistance, each of which was unaware of the identity of the others—each of which was responsible for inciting revolt against the Empire when it finally made itself manifest.

There had been other leaders, but many were killed when the Empire's first Death Star annihilated the planet Alderaan. Leia's adopted father died in that calamity.

Mon Mothma went underground. She joined her political cells with the thousands of guerrillas and insurgents the Empire's cruel dictatorship had spawned. Thousands more joined this Rebel Alliance. Mon Mothma became the acknowledged leader of all the galaxy's creatures who had been left homeless by the Emperor. Homeless, but not without hope.

She traversed the room, now, to the holographic display where she conferred with her two chief advisors, General Madine and Admiral Ackbar. Madine was Corellian—tough, resourceful, if a bit of a martinet. Ackbar was pure Calamarian—a gentle, salmon-colored creature, with huge, sad eyes set in a high-domed head, and webbed hands that made him more at home in water or free space than on board a ship. But if the humans were the arm of the Rebellion, the Calamarians were the soul—which isn't to say they couldn't fight with the best, when pushed to the limit. And the evil Empire had reached that limit.

Lando Calrissian made his way through the crowd, now, scanning faces. He saw Wedge, who was to be his wing pilot—they nodded at each other, gave the thumbs-up sign; but then Lando moved on. Wedge wasn't the one he was looking for. He made it to a clearing near the center, peered around, finally saw his friends standing by a side door. He smiled and wandered over.

Han, Chewie, Leia, and the two droids greeted Lando's appearance with a cacophony of cheers, laughs, beeps, and barks.

"Well, look at you," Solo chided, straightening the lapel of Calrissian's new uniform and pulling on the insignias: "A general!"

Lando laughed affectionately. "I'm a man of many faces and many costumes. Someone must have told them about my little maneuver at the battle of Taanab." Taanab was an agrarian planet raided seasonally by bandits from Norulac. Calrissian—before his stint as governor of Cloud City—had wiped out the bandits against all odds, using legendary flying and unheard of strategies. And he'd done it on a bet.

Han opened his eyes wide with sarcasm. "Hey, don't look at me. I just told them you were a 'fair' pilot. I had no idea they were looking for someone to lead this crazy attack."

"That's all right, I asked for it. I *want* to lead this attack." For one thing, he *liked* dressing up like a general. People gave him the respect he deserved, and he didn't have to give up flying circles around some pompous Imperial military policeman. And that was the other thing—he was finally going to stick it to this Imperial navy, stick it so it hurt, for all the times he'd been stuck. Stick it and leave his signature on it. *General* Calrissian, thank you.

Solo looked at his old friend, admiration combined with disbelief. "Have you ever seen one of those Death Stars? You're in for a very short generalship, old buddy."

"I'm surprised they didn't ask you to do it," Lando smiled.

"Maybe they did," Han intimated. "But I'm not crazy. You're the respectable one, remember? Baron-Administrator of the Bespin Cloud City?"

Leia moved closer to Solo and took his arm protectively. "Han is going to stay on the command ship with me...we're both very grateful for what you're doing, Lando. And proud."

Suddenly, at the center of the room, Mon Mothma signaled for attention. The room fell silent. Anticipation was keen.

"The data brought to us by the Bothan spies have been confirmed," the supreme leader announced. "The Emperor has made a critical error, and the time for our attack has come."

This caused a great stir in the room. As if her message had been a valve letting off pressure, the air hissed with comment. She turned to the hologram of the Death Star, and went on. "We now have the exact location of the Emperor's new battle station. The weapon systems on this Death Star are not yet operational. With the Imperial fleet spread throughout the galaxy in a vain effort to engage us, it is relatively unprotected." She paused here, to let her next statement register its full effect. "Most important, we have learned the Emperor himself is personally overseeing the construction."

A volley of spirited chatter erupted from the assembly. This was it. The chance. The hope no one could hope to hope for. A shot at the Emperor.

Mon Mothma continued when the hubbub died down slightly. "His trip was undertaken in the utmost secrecy, but he underestimated our spy network. Many Bothans died to bring us this information." Her voice turned suddenly stern again to remind them of the price of this enterprise.

Admiral Ackbar stepped forward. His specialty was Imperial defense procedures. He raised his fin and pointed at the holographic model of the force field emanating from Endor. "Although uncompleted, the Death Star is not entirely without a defense mechanism," he instructed in soothing Calamarian tones. "It is protected by an energy shield which is generated by the nearby Moon of Endor, here. No ship can fly through it, no weapon can penetrate it." He stopped for a long moment. He wanted the information to sink in. When he thought it had, he spoke more slowly.

"The shield must be deactivated if *any* attack is to be attempted. Once the shield is down, the cruisers will create a perimeter while the fighters fly into the superstructure, here...and attempt to hit the main reactor..." he pointed to the unfinished portion of the Death Star "...somewhere in here."

Another murmur swept over the room of commanders, like a swell in a heavy sea.

Ackbar concluded. "General Calrissian will lead the fighter attack."

Han turned to Lando, his doubts gilded with respect. "Good luck, buddy."

"Thanks," said Lando simply.

"You're gonna need it."

Admiral Ackbar yielded the floor to General Madine, who was in charge of covert operations. "We have acquired a small Imperial shuttle," Madine declared smugly. "Under this guise, a strike team will land on the moon and deactivate the shield generator. The control bunker is well guarded, but a small squad should be able to penetrate its security."

This news stimulated another round of general mumbling.

Leia turned to Han and said under her breath, "I wonder who they found to pull that one off?"

Madine called out: "General Solo, is your strike team assembled?"

Leia looked up at Han, shock quickly melting to joyous admiration. She knew there was a reason she loved him—in spite of his usual crass insensitivity and oafish bravado. Beneath it all, he had heart.

Moreover, a change *had* come over him since he emerged from carbonization. He wasn't just a loner anymore, only in this for the money. He had lost his selfish edge and had somehow, subtly, become part of the whole. He was actually doing something for someone else, now, and that fact moved Leia greatly. Madine had called him *General*; that meant Han had let himself officially become a member of the army. A part of the whole.

Solo responded to Madine. "My squad is ready, sir, but I need a command crew for the shuttle." He looked questioningly at Chewbacca, and spoke in a lower voice. "It's gonna be rough, old pal. I didn't want to speak for you."

"Roo roowfl," Chewie shook his head with gruff love, and raised his hairy paw.

"That's one," Han called.

"Here's two!" Leia shouted, sticking her arm in the air. Then softly, to Solo: "I'm not letting you out of my sight again, Your Generalship."

"And I'm with you, too!" a voice was raised from the back of the room.

They all turned their heads to see Luke standing at the top of the stairs.

Cheers went up for the last of the Jedi.

And though it wasn't his style, Han was unable to conceal his joy. "That's three," he smiled.

Leia ran up to Luke and hugged him warmly. She felt a special closeness to him all of a sudden, which she attributed to the gravity of the moment, the import of their mission. But then she sensed a change in him, too, a difference of substance that seemed to radiate from his very core—something that she alone could see.

"What is it, Luke?" she whispered. She suddenly wanted to hold him; she could not have said why.

"Nothing. I'll tell you someday," he murmured quietly. It was distinctly not nothing, though.

"All right," she answered, not pushing. "I'll wait." She wondered. Maybe he was just dressed differently—that was probably it. Suited up all in black now—it made him look older. Older, that was it.

Han, Chewie, Lando, Wedge, and several others crowded around Luke all at once, with greetings and diverse sorts of hubbub. The assembly as a whole broke up into multiple such small groups. It was a time for last farewells and good graces.

Artoo beeped a singsong little observation to a somewhat less sanguine Threepio.

"I don't think 'exciting' is the right word," the golden droid answered. Being a translator in his master program, of course, Threepio was most concerned with locating the right word to describe the present situation.

The *Millennium Falcon* rested in the main docking bay of the Rebel Star Cruiser, getting loaded and serviced. Just beyond it sat the stolen Imperial shuttle, looking anomalous in the midst of all the Rebel X-wing fighters.

Chewie supervised the final transfer of weapons and supplies to the shuttle and oversaw the placement of the strike team. Han stood with Lando between the two ships, saying good-bye—for all they knew, forever.

"I mean it, take her!" Solo insisted, indicating the *Falcon*. "She'll bring you luck. You *know* she's the fastest ship in the whole fleet, now." Han had really souped her up after winning her from Lando. She'd always been fast, but now she was much faster. And the modifications Solo added had really made the *Falcon* a part of him—he'd put his love and sweat into it. His spirit. So giving her to Lando now was truly Solo's final transformation—as selfless a gift as he'd ever given.

And Lando understood. "Thanks, old buddy. I'll take good care of her. *You* know I always flew her better than you did, anyway. She won't get a scratch on her, with me at the stick."

Solo looked warmly at the endearing rogue. "I've got your word—not a scratch."

"Take off, you pirate—next thing you'll have me putting down a security deposit."

"See you soon, pal."

They parted without their true feelings expressed aloud, as was the way between men of deeds in those times; each walked up the ramp into a different ship.

Han entered the cockpit of the Imperial shuttle as Luke was doing some fine tuning on a rear navigator panel. Chewbacca, in the copilot's seat, was trying to figure out the Imperial controls. Han took the pilot's chair, and Chewie growled grumpily about the design.

"Yeah, yeah," Solo answered, "I don't think the Empire designed it with a Wookiee in mind."

Leia walked in from the hold, taking her seat near Luke. "We're all set back there."

"Rrrwfr," said Chewie, hitting the first sequence of switches. He looked over at Solo, but Han was motionless, staring out the window at something. Chewie and Leia both followed his gaze to the object of his unyielding attention—the *Millennium Falcon*.

Leia gently nudged the pilot. "Hey, you awake up there?"

"I just got a funny feeling," Han mused. "Like I'm not going to see her again." He thought of the times she'd saved him with her speed, of the times he'd saved her with his cunning, or his touch. He thought of the universe they'd seen together, of the shelter she'd given him; of the way he knew her, inside and out. Of the times they'd slept in each other's embrace, floating still as a quiet dream in the black silence of deep space.

Chewbacca, hearing this, took his own longing look at the *Falcon*. Leia put her hand on Solo's shoulder. She knew he had special love for his ship and was reluctant to interrupt this last communion. But time was dear, and becoming dearer. "Come on, Captain," she whispered. "Let's move."

Han snapped back to the moment. "Right. Okay, Chewie, let's find out what this baby can do."

They fired up the engines in the stolen shuttle, eased out of the docking bay, and banked off into the endless night.

Construction on the Death Star proceeded. Traffic in the area was thick with transport ships, TIE fighters and equipment shuttles. Periodically, the Super Star Destroyer orbited the area, surveying progress on the space station from every angle.

The bridge of the Star Destroyer was a hive of activity. Messengers ran back and forth along a string of controllers studying their tracking screens, monitoring ingress and egress of vehicles through the deflector shield. Codes were sent and received, orders given, diagrams plotted. It was an operation involving a thousand scurrying ships, and everything was proceeding with maximum efficiency, until Controller Jhoff made contact with a shuttle of the Lambda class, approaching the shield from Sector Seven.

"Shuttle to Control, please come in," the voice broke into Jhoff's headset with the normal amount of static.

"We have you on our screen now," the controller replied into his comlink. "Please identify."

"This is Shuttle *Tydirium*, requesting deactivation of the deflector shield."

"Shuttle *Tydirium*, transmit the clearance code for shield passage."

Up in the shuttle, Han threw a worried look at the others and said into his comlink, "Transmission commencing."

Chewie flipped a bank of switches, producing a syncopated series of high-frequency transmission noises.

Leia bit her lip, bracing herself for fight or flight. "Now we find out if that code was worth the price we paid."

Chewie whined nervously.

Luke stared at the huge Super Star Destroyer that loomed everywhere in front of them. It fixed his eye with its glittering darkness, filled his vision like a malignant cataract—but it made more than his vision opaque. It filled his mind with blackness, too; and his heart. Black fear, and a special knowing. "Vader is on that ship," he whispered.

"You're just jittery, Luke," Han reassured them all. "There are lots of command ships. But, Chewie," he cautioned, "let's keep our distance, without looking like we're keeping our distance."

"Awroff rwrgh rrfrough?"

"I don't know—fly casual," Han barked back.

"They're taking a long time with that code clearance," Leia said tightly. What if it didn't work? The

Alliance could do nothing if the Empire's deflector
shield remained functioning. Leia tried to clear her
mind, tried to focus on the shield generator she wanted
to reach, tried to weed away all feelings of doubt or
fear she may have been giving off.

"I'm endangering the mission," Luke spoke now, in
a kind of emotional resonance with his secret sister.
His thoughts were of Vader, though: their father. "I
shouldn't have come."

Han tried to buoy things up. "Hey, why don't we
try to be optimistic about this?" He felt beleaguered
by negativity.

"He knows I'm here," Luke avowed. He kept staring
at the command ship out the view-window. It seemed
to taunt him. It awaited.

"Come on, kid, you're imagining things."

"Ararh gragh," Chewie mumbled. Even he was grim.

Lord Vader stood quite still, staring out a large view-
screen at the Death Star. He thrilled to the sight of this
monument to the dark side of the Force. Icily he ca-
ressed it with his gaze.

Like a floating ornament, it sparkled for him. A magic
globe. Tiny specks of light raced across its surface,
mesmerizing the Dark Lord as if he were a small child
entranced by a special toy. It was a transcendant state
he was in, a moment of heightened perceptions.

And then, all at once, in the midst of the stillness
of his contemplation, he grew absolutely motionless:
not a breath, not even a heartbeat stirred to mar his
concentration. He strained his every sense into the
ether. What had he felt? His spirit tilted its head to
listen. Some echo, some vibration apprehended only
by him, had passed—no, had not passed. Had swirled
the moment and altered the very shape of things. Things
were no longer the same.

He walked down the row of controllers until he came
to the spot where Admiral Piett was leaning over the
tracking screen of Controller Jhoff. Piett straightened
at Vader's approach, then bowed stiffly, at the neck.

"Where is that shuttle going?" Vader demanded quietly, without preliminary.

Piett turned back to the view-screen and spoke into the comlink. "Shuttle *Tydirium*, what is your cargo and destination?"

The filtered voice of the shuttle pilot came back over the receiver. "Parts and technical personnel for the Sanctuary Moon."

The bridge commander looked to Vader for a reaction. He hoped nothing was amiss. Lord Vader did not take mistakes lightly.

"Do they have a code clearance?" Vader questioned.

"It's an older code, but it checks out," Piett replied immediately. "I was about to clear them." There was no point in lying to the Lord of the Sith. He always knew if you lied; lies sang out to the Dark Lord.

"I have a strange feeling about that ship," Vader said more to himself than to anyone else.

"Should I hold them?" Piett hurried, anxious to please his master.

"No, let them pass, I will deal with this myself."

"As you wish, my Lord." Piett bowed, partly to hide his surprise. He nodded at Controller Jhoff, who spoke into the comlink, to the Shuttle *Tydirium*.

In the Shuttle *Tydirium*, the group waited tensely. The more questions they were asked about things like cargo and destination, the more likely it seemed they were going to blow their cover.

Han looked fondly at his old Wookiee partner. "Chewie, if they don't go for this, we're gonna have to beat it quick." It was a good-bye speech, really; they all knew this pokey shuttle wasn't about to outrun anything in the neighborhood.

The static voice of the controller broke up, and then came in clearly over the comlink. "Shuttle *Tydirium*, deactivation of the shield will commence immediately. Follow your present course."

Everyone but Luke exhaled in simultaneous relief; as if the trouble were all over now, instead of just beginning. Luke continued to stare at the command ship, as if engaged in some silent, complex dialogue.

Chewie barked loudly.

"Hey, what did I tell you?" Han grinned. "No sweat."

Leia smiled affectionately. "Is that what you told us?"

Solo pushed the throttle forward, and the stolen shuttle moved smoothly toward the green Sanctuary Moon.

Vader, Piett, and Jhoff watched the view-screen in the control room, as the weblike deflector grid read-out parted to admit the Shuttle *Tydirium*, which moved slowly toward the center of the web—to Endor.

Vader turned to the deck officer and spoke with more urgency in his voice than was usually heard. "Ready my shuttle. I must go to the Emperor."

Without waiting for response, the Dark Lord strode off, clearly in the thrall of a dark thought.

 5

THE trees of Endor stood a thousand feet tall. Their
trunks, covered with shaggy, rust bark, rose straight as
a pillar, some of them as big around as a house, some
thin as a leg. Their foliage was spindly, but lush in
color, scattering the sunlight in delicate blue-green
patterns over the forest floor.

Distributed thickly among these ancient giants was
the usual array of woodsy flora—pines of several species, various deciduous forms, variously gnarled and
leafy. The groundcover was primarily fern, but so dense
in spots as to resemble a gentle green sea that rippled
softly in the forest breeze.

This was the entire moon: verdant, primeval, silent.
Light filtered through the sheltering branches like
golden ichor, as if the very air were alive. It was warm,
and it was cool. This was Endor.

The stolen Imperial shuttle sat in a clearing many
miles from the Imperial landing port, camouflaged with
a blanket of dead branches, leaves, and mulch. In addition the little ship was thoroughly dwarfed by the
towering trees. Its steely hull might have looked in-

congruous here, had it not been so totally inconspic-
uous.

On the hill adjacent to the clearing, the Rebel con-
tingent was just beginning to make its way up a steep
trail. Leia, Chewie, Han, and Luke led the way, followed in single file by the raggedy, helmeted squad
of the strike team. This unit was composed of the elite
groundfighters of the Rebel Alliance. A scruffy bunch
in some ways, they'd each been hand-picked for ini-
tiative, cunning, and ferocity. Some were trained commandos, some paroled criminals—but they all hated
the Empire with a passion that exceeded self-preser-
vation. And they all knew this was the crucial raid. If
they failed to destroy the shield generator here, the
Rebellion was doomed. No second chances.

Consequently, no one had to tell them to be alert
as they made their way silently up the forest path. They
were, every one, more alert than they had ever been.

Artoo-Detoo and See-Threepio brought up the rear
of the brigade. Artoo's domed pate swiveled 'round and
'round as he went, blinking his sensor lights at the
infinitely tall trees which surrounded them.

"Beee-doop!" he commented to Threepio.

"No, I don't think it's pretty here," his golden companion replied testily. "With our luck, it's inhabited
solely by droid-eating monsters."

The trooper just ahead of Threepio turned around
and gave them a harsh "Shush!"

Threepio turned back to Artoo, and whispered,
"Quiet, Artoo."

They were all a bit nervous.

Up ahead, Chewie and Leia reached the crest of the
hill. They dropped to the ground, crawled the last few
feet, and peered over the edge. Chewbacca raised his
great paw, signaling the rest of the group to stop. All
at once, the forest seemed to become much more silent.

Luke and Han crawled forward on their bellies, to
view what the others were observing. Pointing through
the ferns, Chewie and Leia cautioned stealth. Not far
below, in a glen beside a clear pool, two Imperial scouts

had set up temporary camp. They were fixing a meal of rations and were preoccupied warming it over a portable cooker. Two speeder bikes were parked nearby.

"Should we try to go around?" whispered Leia.

"It'll take time," Luke shook his head.

Han peeked from behind a rock. "Yeah, and if they catch sight of us and report, this whole party's for nothing."

"Is it just the two of them?" Leia still sounded skeptical.

"Let's take a look," smiled Luke, with a sigh of tension about to be released; they all responded with a similar grin. It was beginning.

Leia motioned the rest of the squad to remain where they were; then she, Luke, Han, and Chewbacca quietly edged closer to the scout camp.

When they were quite near the clearing, but still covered by underbrush, Solo slid quickly to the lead position. "Stay here," he rasped, "Chewie and I will take care of this." He flashed them his most roguish smile.

"Quietly," warned Luke, "there might be—"

But before he could finish, Han jumped up with his furry partner and rushed into the clearing.

"—more out there," Luke finished speaking to himself. He looked over at Leia.

She shrugged. "What'd you expect?" Some things never changed.

Before Luke could respond, though, they were distracted by a loud commotion in the glen. They flattened to the ground and watched.

Han was engaged in a rousing fist fight with one of the scouts—he hadn't looked so happy in days. The other scout jumped on his speeder bike to escape. But by the time he'd ignited the engines, Chewie was able to get off a few shots from his crossbow laser. The ill-fated scout crashed instantly against an enormous tree; a brief, muffled explosion followed.

Leia drew her laser pistol and raced into the battle zone, followed closely by Luke. As soon as they were running clear, though, several large laser blasts went off all around them, tumbling them to the ground. Leia lost her gun.

Dazed, they both looked up to see two more Imperial scouts emerge from the far side of the clearing, heading for their speeder bikes hidden in the peripheral foliage. The scouts holstered their pistols as they mounted the bikes and fired up the engines.

Leia staggered to her feet, "Over there, two more of them!"

"I see 'em," answered Luke, rising. "Stay here."

But Leia had ideas of her own. She ran to the remaining rocket speeder, charged it up, and took off in pursuit of the fleeing scouts. As she tore past Luke, he jumped up behind her on the bike, and off they flew.

"Quick, center switch," he shouted to her over her shoulder, over the roar of the rocket engines. "Jam their comlinks!"

As Luke and Leia soared out of the clearing after the Imperials, Han and Chewie were just subduing the last scout. "Hey, wait!" Solo shouted; but they were gone. He threw his weapon to the ground in frustration, and the rest of the Rebel commando squad poured over the rise into the clearing.

Luke and Leia sped through the dense foliage, a few feet off the ground, Leia at the controls, Luke grabbing on behind her. The two escaping Imperial scouts had a good lead, but at two hundred miles per hour, Leia was the better pilot—the talent ran in her family.

She let off a burst from the speeder's laser cannon periodically, but was still too far behind to be very accurate. The explosions hit away from the moving targets, splintering trees and setting the shrubbery afire, as the bikes weaved in and out between massive, imposing branches.

"Move closer!" Luke shouted.

Leia opened the throttle, closed the gap. The two scouts sensed their pursuer gaining and recklessly veered this way and that, skimming through a narrow opening between two trees. One of the bikes scraped the bark, tipping the scout almost out of control, slowing him significantly.

"Get alongside!" Luke yelled into Leia's ear.

She pulled her speeder so close to the scout's, their steering vanes scraped hideously against each other. Luke suddenly leaped from the back of Leia's bike to the back of the scout's, grabbed the Imperial warrior around the neck, and flipped him off. The white-armored trooper smashed into a thick trunk with a bone-shattering crunch, and settled forever into the sea of ferns.

Luke scooted forward to the driver's seat of the speeder bike, played with the controls a few seconds, and lurched forward, following Leia, who'd pulled ahead. The two of them now tore after the remaining scout.

Over hill and under stonebridge they flew, narrowly avoiding collision, flaming dry vines in their afterburn. The chase swung north and passed a gully where two more Imperial scouts were resting. A moment later, *they* swung into pursuit, now hot on Luke and Leia's tail, blasting away with laser cannon. Luke, still behind Leia took a glancing blow.

"Keep on that one!" he shouted up at her, indicating the scout in the lead. "I'll take the two behind us!"

Leia shot ahead. Luke, at the same instant, flared up his retrorockets, slamming the bike into rapid deceleration. The two scouts on his tail zipped past him in a blur on either side, unable to slow their momentum. Luke immediately roared into high velocity again, firing with his blasters, suddenly in pursuit of his pursuers.

His third round hit its mark: one of the scouts, blown out of control, went spinning against a boulder in a rumble of flame.

The scout's cohort took a single glance at the flash, and put his bike into supercharge mode, speeding even faster. Luke kept pace.

Far ahead, Leia and the first scout continued their own high-speed slalom through the barricades of im-

passive trunks and low-slung branches. She had to brake
through so many turns, in fact, Leia seemed unable to
draw any closer to her quarry. Suddenly she shot into
the air, at an unbelievably steep incline, and quickly
vanished from sight.

The scout turned in confusion, uncertain whether
to relax or cringe at his pursuer's sudden disappear-
ance. Her whereabouts became clear soon enough. Out
of the tree-tops, Leia dove down on him, cannon blasting from above. The scout's bike took the shock wave
from a near hit. Her speed was even greater than she'd
anticipated, and in a moment she was racing alongside
him. But before she knew what was happening, he
reached down and drew a handgun from his holster—
and before she could react, he fired.

Her bike spun out of control. She jumped free just
in time—the speeder exploded on a giant tree, as Leia
rolled clear into a tangle of matted vines, rotting logs,
shallow water. The last thing she saw was the orange
fireball through a cloud of smoking greenery; and then
blackness.

The scout looked behind him at the explosion, with
a satisfied sneer. When he faced forward again, though,
the smug look faded, for he was on a collision course
with a fallen tree. In a moment it was all over but the
flaming.

Meanwhile, Luke was closing fast on the last scout.
As they wove from tree to tree, Luke eased up behind
and then drew even with the Imperial rider. The fleeing
soldier suddenly swerved, slamming his bike into
Luke's—they both tipped precariously, barely missing
a large fallen trunk in their path. The scout zoomed
under it, Luke over it—and when he came down on
the other side, he crashed directly on top of the scout's
vehicle. Their steering vanes locked.

The bikes were shaped more or less like one-man
sleds, with long thin rods extending from their snouts,
and fluttery ailerons for guidance at the tip of the rods.
With these vanes locked, the bikes flew as one, though
either rider could steer.

The scout banked hard right, to try to smash Luke into an onrushing grove of saplings on the right. But at the last second Luke leaned all his weight left, turning the locked speeders actually horizontal, with Luke on top, the scout on the bottom.

The biker scout suddenly stopped resisting Luke's leftward leaning and threw his own weight in the same direction, resulting in the bikes flipping over three hundred sixty degrees and coming to rest exactly upright once more... but with an enormous tree looming immediately in front of Luke.

Without thinking, he leaped from his bike. A fraction of a second later, the scout veered steeply left—the steering vanes separated—and Luke's riderless speeder crashed explosively into the redwood.

Luke rolled, decelerating, up a moss-covered slope. The scout swooped high, circled around, and came looking for him.

Luke stumbled out of the bushes as the speeder was bearing down on him full throttle, laser cannon firing. Luke ignited his lightsaber and stood his ground. His weapon deflected every bolt the scout fired at Luke; but the bike kept coming. In a few moments, the two would meet; the bike accelerated even more, intent on bodily slicing the young Jedi in half. At the last moment, though, Luke stepped aside—with perfect timing, like a master matador facing a rocket-powered bull—and chopped off the bike's steering vanes with a single mighty slash of his lightsaber.

The bike quickly began to shudder; then pitch and roll. In a second it was out of control entirely, and in another second it was a rumbling billow of fire on the forest floor.

Luke snuffed out his lightsaber and headed back to join the others.

Vader's shuttle swung around the unfinished portion of the Death Star and settled fluidly into the main docking bay. Soundless bearings lowered the Dark Lord's ramp; soundless were his feet as they glided down the chilly steel. Chill with purpose were his strides, and swift.

The main corridor was filled with courtiers, all awaiting an audience with the Emperor. Vader curled his lip at them—fools, all. Pompous toadys in their velvet robes and painted faces; perfumed bishops passing notes and passing judgments among themselves—for who else cared; oily favor-merchants, bent low from the weight of jewelry still warm from a previous owner's dying flesh; easy, violent men and women, lusting to be tampered with.

Vader had no patience for such petty filth. He passed them without a nod, though many of them would have paid dearly for a felicitous glance from the high Dark Lord.

When he reached the elevator to the Emperor's tower, he found the door closed. Red-robed, heavily armed royal guards flanked the shaft, seemingly unaware of Vader's presence. Out of the shadow, an officer stepped forward, directly in Lord Vader's path, preventing his further approach.

"You may not enter," the officer said evenly.

Vader did not waste words. He raised his hand, fingers outstretched, toward the officer's throat. Ineffably, the officer began to choke. His knees started buckling, his face turned ashen.

Gasping for air, he spoke again. "It is the... Emperor's...command."

Like a spring, Vader released the man from his remote grip. The officer, breathing again, sank to the floor, trembling. He rubbed his neck gently.

"I will await his convenience," Vader said. He turned and looked out the view window. Leaf-green Endor glowed there, floating in black space, almost as if it were radiant from some internal source of energy. He felt its pull like a magnet, like a vacuum, like a torch in the dead night.

Han and Chewie crouched opposite each other in the forest clearing, being quiet, being near. The rest

Darth Vader in the
Docking Bay of the new Death Star.

C-3PO on the Sail Barge with members of Jabba's court.

Princess Leia enslaved by Jabba the Hutt.

Lando Calrissian struggling with one of the skiff guards.

Above, Yoda

Right, Salacious
    Crumb

Below, An Ewok

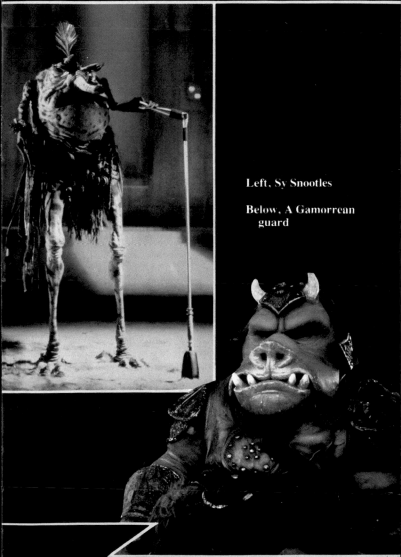

Left, Sy Snootles

Below, A Gamorrean guard

Admiral Ackbar and one of the Mon Calamari.

Lando Calrissian, Chewbacca, and Han Solo in the Rebel Briefing Room.

Luke and Leia in the Ewok village.

Han, Leia, and Chewie captured by Stormtroopers.

R2-D2 and Wicket

of the strike squad relaxed—as much as was possible—spread out around them in groups of twos and threes. They all waited.

Even Threepio was silent. He sat beside Artoo, polishing his fingers for lack of anything better to do. The others checked their watches, or their weapons, as the afternoon sunlight ticked away.

Artoo sat, unmoving except for the little radar screen that stuck out the top of his blue and silver dome, revolving, scanning the forest. He exuded the calm patience of a utilized function, a program being run.

Suddenly, he beeped.

Threepio ceased his obsessive polishing and looked apprehensively into the forest. "Someone's coming," he translated.

The rest of the squad faced out; weapons were raised. A twig cracked beyond the western perimeter. No one breathed.

With a weary stride, Luke stepped out of the foliage, into the clearing. All relaxed, lowered their guns. Luke was too tired to care. He plopped down on the hard dirt beside Solo and lay back with an exhausted groan.

"Hard day, huh kid?" Han commented.

Luke sat up on one elbow, smiling. It seemed like an awful lot of effort and noise just to nail a couple of Imperial scouts; and they hadn't even gotten to the really tough part yet. But Han could still maintain his light tone. It was a state of grace, his particular brand of charm. Luke hoped it never vanished from the universe. "Wait'll we get to that generator," he retorted in kind.

Solo looked around, into the forest Luke had just come from. "Where's Leia?"

Luke's face suddenly turned to one of concern. "She didn't come back?"

"I thought she was with you," Han's voice marginally rose in pitch and volume.

"We got split up," Luke explained. He exchanged a grim look with Solo, then both of them slowly stood. "We better look for her."

"Don't you want to rest a while?" Han suggested. He could see the fatigue in Luke's face and wanted to spare him for the coming confrontation, which would surely take more strength than any of them had.

"I want to find Leia," he said softly.

Han nodded, without argument. He signaled to the Rebel officer who was second in command of the strike squad. The officer ran up and saluted.

"Take the squad ahead," ordered Solo. "We'll rendezvous at the shield generator at 0-30."

The officer saluted again and immediately organized the troops. Within a minute they were filing silently into the forest, greatly relieved to be moving at last.

Luke, Chewbacca, General Solo, and the two droids faced in the opposite direction. Artoo led the way, his revolving scanner sensing for all the parameters that described his mistress; and the others followed him into the woods.

The first thing Leia was aware of was her left elbow. It was wet. It was lying in a pool of water, getting quite soaked.

She moved the elbow out of the water with a little splash, revealing something else: pain—pain in her entire arm when it moved. For the time being, she decided to keep it still.

The next thing to enter her consciousness were sounds. The splash her elbow had made, the rustle of leaves, an occasional bird chirp. Forest sounds. With a grunt, she took a short breath and noted the grunting sound.

Smells began to fill her nostrils next: humid mossy smells, leafy oxygen smells, the odor of a distant honey, the vapor of rare flowers.

Taste came with smell—the taste of blood on her tongue. She opened and closed her mouth a few times, to localize where the blood was coming from; but she couldn't. Instead, the attempt only brought the recognition of new pains—in her head, in her neck, in her back. She started to move her arms again, but this entailed a whole catalogue of new pains; so once again, she rested.

Next she allowed temperature to waft into her sensorium. Sun warmed the fingers of her right hand, while the palm, in shadow, stayed cool. A breeze drafted the back of her legs. Her left hand, pressed against the skin of her belly, was warm.

She felt...awake.

Slowly—reticent actually to witness the damage, since seeing things made them real, and seeing her own broken body was not a reality she wanted to acknowledge—slowly, she opened her eyes. Things were blurry here at ground level. Hazy browns and grays in the foreground, becoming progressively brighter and greener in the distance. Slowly, things came into focus.

Slowly, she saw the Ewok.

A strange, small, furry creature, he stood three feet from Leia's face and no more than three feet tall. He had large, dark, curious, brownish eyes, and stubby little finger-paws. Completely covered, head to foot, with soft, brown fur, he looked like nothing so much as the stuffed baby Wookiee doll Leia remembered playing with as a child. In fact, when she first saw the creature standing before her, she thought it merely a dream, a childhood memory rising out of her addled brain.

But this wasn't a dream. It was an Ewok. And his name was Wicket.

Nor was he exclusively cute—for as Leia focused further, she could see a knife strapped to his waist. It was all he wore, save for a thin leather mantle only covering his head.

They watched each other, unmoving, for a long minute. The Ewok seemed puzzled by the princess; uncertain of what she was, or what she intended. At the moment, Leia intended to see if she could sit up.

She sat up, with a groan.

The sound apparently frightened the little fluffball; he rapidly stumbled backward, tripped, and fell. "Eeeeep!" he squeaked.

Leia scrutinized herself closely, looking for signs of serious damage. Her clothes were torn; she had cuts, bruises, and scrapes everywhere—but nothing seemed to be broken or irreparable. On the other hand, she had no idea where she was. She groaned again.

That did it for the Ewok. He jumped up, grabbed a four-foot-long spear, and held it defensively in her direction. Warily, he circled, poking the pointed javelin at her, clearly more fearful than aggressive.

"Hey, cut that out," Leia brushed the weapon away with annoyance. That was all she needed now—to be skewered by a teddy bear. More gently, she added: "I'm not going to hurt you."

Gingerly, she stood up, testing her legs. The Ewok backed away with caution.

"Don't be afraid," Leia tried to put reassurance into her voice. "I just want to see what happened to my bike here." She knew the more she talked in this tone, the more at ease it would put the little creature. Moreover, she knew if she was talking, she was doing okay.

Her legs were a little unsteady, but she was able to walk slowly over to the charred remains of the speeder, now lying in a half-melted pile at the base of the partially blackened tree.

Her movement was away from the Ewok, who, like a skittish puppy, took this as a safe sign and followed her to the wreckage. Leia picked the Imperial scout's laser pistol off the ground; it was all that was left of him.

"I think I got off at the right time," she muttered.

The Ewok appraised the scene with his big, shiny eyes, nodded, shook his head, and squeaked vociferously for several seconds.

Leia looked all around her at the dense forest, then sat down, with a sigh, on a fallen log. She was at eye-level with the Ewok, now, and they once again regarded each other, a little bewildered, a little concerned. "Trouble is, I'm sort of stuck here," she confided. "And I don't even know where here is."

She put her head in her hands, partly to mull over the situation, partly to rub some of the soreness from her temples. Wicket sat down beside her and mimicked her posture exactly—head in paws, elbows on knees—then let out a little sympathetic Ewok sigh.

Leia laughed appreciatively and scratched the small creature's furry head, between the ears. He purred like a kitten.

"You wouldn't happen to have a comlink on you by any chance?" Big joke—but she hoped maybe talking about it would give her an idea. The Ewok blinked a few times—but he only gave her a mystified look. Leia smiled. "No, I guess not."

Suddenly Wicket froze; his ears twitched, and he sniffed the air. He tilted his head in an attitude of keen attention.

"What is it?" Leia whispered. Something was obviously amiss. Then she heard it: a quiet snap in the bushes beyond, a tentative rustling.

All at once the Ewok let out a loud, terrified screech. Leia drew her pistol, jumping behind the log; Wicket scurried beside her and squeezed under it. A long silence followed. Tense, uncertain, Leia trained her senses on the near underbrush. Ready to fight.

For all her readiness, she hadn't expected the laser bolt to come from where it did—high, off to the right. It exploded in front of the log with a shower of light and pine needles. She returned the fire quickly—two short blasts—then just as quickly sensed something behind her. Slowly she swiveled, to find an Imperial scout standing over her, his weapon leveled at her head. He reached out his hand for the pistol she held.

"I'll take that," he ordered.

Without warning, a furry hand came out from under the log and jabbed the scout in the leg with a knife. The man howled in pain, began jumping about on one foot.

Leia dove for his fallen laser pistol. She rolled, fired

and hit the scout squarely in the chest, flash-burning his heart.

Quickly the forest was quiet once more, the noise and light swallowed up as if they had never been. Leia lay still where she was, panting softly, waiting for another attack. None came.

Wicket poked his fuzzy head up from under the log, and looked around. "Eeep rrp scrp ooooh," he mumbled in a tone of awe.

Leia hopped up, ran all about the area, crouched, turned her head from side to side. It seemed safe for the time being. She motioned to her chubby new friend. "Come on, we'd better get out of here."

As they moved into the thick flora, Wicket took the lead. Leia was unsure at first, but he shrieked urgently at her and tugged her sleeve. So she relinquished control to the odd little beast and followed him.

She cast her mind adrift for a while, letting her feet carry her nimbly along among the gargantuan trees. She was struck, suddenly, not by the smallness of the Ewok who guided her, but by her own smallness next to these trees. They were ten thousand years old, some of them, and tall beyond sight. They were temples to the life-force she championed; they reached out to the rest of the universe. She felt herself part of their greatness, but also dwarfed by it.

And lonely. She felt lonely here, in this forest of giants. All her life she'd lived among giants of her own people: her father, the great Senator Organa; her mother, then Minister of Education; her peers and friends, giants all...

But these trees. They were like mighty exclamation points, announcing their own preeminence. They were here! They were older than time! They would be here long after Leia was gone, after the Rebellion, after the Empire...

And then she didn't feel lonely again, but felt a part again, of these magnificent, poised beings. A part of them across time, and space, connected by the vibrant, vital force, of which...

It was confusing. A part, and apart. She couldn't grasp it. She felt large and small, brave and timid. She felt like a tiny, creative spark, dancing about in the fires of life...dancing behind a furtive, pudgy midget bear, who kept beckoning her deeper into the woods.

It was this, then, that the Alliance was fighting to preserve—furry creatures in mammoth forests helping scared, brave princesses to safety. Leia wished her parents were alive, so she could tell them.

Lord Vader stepped out of the elevator and stood at the entrance to the throne room. The light-cables hummed either side of the shaft, casting an eerie glow on the royal guards who waited there. He marched resolutely down the walkway, up the stairs, and paused subserviently behind the throne. He kneeled, motionless.

Almost immediately, he heard the Emperor's voice. "Rise. Rise and speak, my friend."

Vader rose, as the throne swiveled around, and the Emperor faced him.

They made eye contact from light-years and a soul's breath away. Across that abyss, Vader responded. "My master, a small Rebel force has penetrated the shield and landed on Endor."

"Yes, I know." There was no hint of surprise in his tone; rather, fulfillment.

Vader noted this, then went on. "My son is with them."

The Emperor's brow furrowed less than a millimeter. His voice remained cool, unruffled, slightly curious. "Are you sure?"

"I felt him, my master." It was almost a taunt. He knew the Emperor was frightened of young Skywalker, afraid of his power. Only together could Vader and the Emperor hope to pull the Jedi Knight over to the dark side. He said it again, emphasizing his own singularity. "*I* felt him."

"Strange, that *I* have not," the Emperor murmured, his eyes becoming slits. They both knew the Force wasn't all-powerful—and no one was infallible with its use. It had everything to do with awareness, with vision. Certainly, Vader and his son were more closely linked than was the Emperor with young Skywalker— but, in addition, the Emperor was now aware of a cross-current he hadn't read before, a buckle in the Force he couldn't quite understand. "I wonder if your feelings on this matter are clear, Lord Vader."

"They are clear, my master." He knew his son's presence, it galled him and fueled him and lured him and howled in a voice of its own.

"Then you must go to the Sanctuary Moon and wait for him," Emperor Palpatine said simply. As long as things were clear, things were clear.

"He will come to me?" Vader asked skeptically. This was not what he felt. He felt drawn.

"Of his own free will," the Emperor assured him. It must be of his own free will, else all was lost. A spirit could not be coerced into corruption, it had to be seduced. It had to participate actively. It had to crave. Luke Skywalker knew these things, and still he circled the black fire, like a cat. Destinies could never be read with absolute certainty—but Skywalker would come, that was clear. "I have foreseen it. His compassion for you will be his undoing." Compassion had always been the weak belly of the Jedi, and forever would be. It was the ultimate vulnerability. The Emperor had none. "The boy will come to you, and you will then bring him before me."

Vader bowed low. "As you wish."

With casual malice, the Emperor dismissed the Dark Lord. With grim anticipation, Vader strode out of the throne room, to board the shuttle for Endor.

Luke, Chewie, Han, and Threepio picked their way methodically through the undergrowth behind Artoo, whose antenna continued to revolve. It was remarkable the way the little droid was able to blaze a trail over jungle terrain like this, but he did it without fuss, the miniature cutting tools on his walkers and dome slicing neatly through anything too dense to push out of the way.

Artoo suddenly stopped, causing some consternation on the part of his followers. His radar screen spun faster, he clicked and whirred to himself, then darted forward with an excited announcement. "Vrrr dEEp dWP booooo dWEE op!"

Threepio raced behind him. "Artoo says the rocket bikes are right up—oh, dear."

They broke into the clearing just ahead of the others, but all stopped in a clump on entering. The charred debris of three speeder bikes was strewn around the area—not to mention the remains of some Imperial scouts.

They spread out to inspect the rubble. Little of note was evident, except a torn piece of Leia's jacket. Han held it soberly, thinking.

Threepio spoke quietly. "Artoo's sensors find no other trace of Princess Leia."

"I hope she's nowhere near here, now," Han said to the trees. He didn't want to imagine her loss. After all that had happened, he simply couldn't believe it would end this way for her.

"Looks like she ran into two of them," Luke said, just to say something. None of them wanted to draw any conclusions.

"She seems to have done all right," Han responded somewhat tersely. He was addressing Luke, but speaking to himself.

Only Chewbacca seemed uninterested in the clearing in which they were standing. He stood facing the dense foliage beyond, then wrinkled his nose, sniffing.

"Rahrr!" he shouted, plunging into the thicket. The others rushed after him.

Artoo whistled softly, nervously.

"Picking up what?" Threepio snapped. "Try to be more specific, would you?"

The trees became significantly taller as the group

pushed on. Not that it was possible to see any higher, but the girth of the trunks was increasingly massive. The rest of the forest was thinning a bit in the process, making passage easier, but giving them the distinct sense that they were shrinking. It was an ominous feeling.

All at once the undergrowth gave way again, to yet another open space. At the center of this clearing, a single tall stake was planted in the ground, from which hung several shanks of raw meat. The searchers stared, then cautiously walked to the stake.

"What's this?" Threepio voiced the collective question.

Chewbacca's nose was going wild, in some kind of olfactory delirium. He held himself back as long as he could, but was finally unable to resist: he reached out for one of the slabs of meat.

"No wait!" shouted Luke. "Don't—"

But it was too late. The moment the meat was pulled from the stake, a huge net sprang up all around the adventurers, instantly hoisting them high above the ground, in a twisting jumble of arms and legs.

Artoo whistled wildly—he was programmed to hate being upside-down—as the Wookiee bayed his regret.

Han peeled a hairy paw away from his mouth, spitting fur. "Great, Chewie. Nice work. Always thinking with your stomach—"

"Take it easy," called Luke. "Let's just figure out how to get out of this thing." He tried, but was unable, to free his arms; one locked behind him through the net, one pinned to Threepio's leg. "Can anyone reach my lightsaber?"

Artoo was bottommost. He extended his cutting appendage and began clipping the loops of the viney net.

Solo, meantime, was trying to squeeze his arm past Threepio, trying to stretch to reach the lightsaber hanging at Luke's waist. They settled, jerkily, as Artoo cut through another piece of mesh, leaving Han pressed face to face with the protocol droid.

"Out of the way, Goldenrod—unh—get off of—"

"How do you think *I* feel?" Threepio charged. There *was* no protocol in a situation like this.

"I don't really—" Han began, but suddenly Artoo cut through the last link, and the entire group crashed out of the net, to the ground. As they gradually regained their senses, sat up, checked to make certain the others were all safe, one by one they realized they were surrounded by twenty furry little creatures, all wearing soft leather hoods, or caps; all brandishing spears.

One came close to Han, pushing a long spear in his face, screeching "eeee wk!"

Solo knocked the weapon aside, with a curt directive. "Point that thing somewhere else."

A second Ewok became alarmed, and lunged at Han. Again, he deflected the spear, but in the process got cut on the arm.

Luke reached for his lightsaber, but just then a third Ewok ran forward, pushing the more aggressive ones out of the way, and shrieked a long string of seeming invective at them, in a decidedly scolding tone. At this, Luke decided to hold off on his lightsaber.

Han was wounded and angry, though. He started to draw his pistol. Luke stopped him before he cleared holster, with a look. "Don't—it'll be all right," he added. Never confuse ability with appearance, Ben used to tell him—or actions with motivations. Luke was uncertain of these little furries, but he had a feeling.

Han held his arm, and held his peace, as the Ewoks swarmed around, confiscating all their weapons. Luke even relinquished his lightsaber. Chewie growled suspiciously.

Artoo and Threepio were just extracting themselves from the collapsed net, as the Ewoks chattered excitedly to each other.

Luke turned to the golden droid. "Threepio, can you understand what they're saying?"

Threepio rose from the mesh trap, feeling himself for dents or rattles. "Oh, my head," he complained.

At the sight of his fully upright body, the Ewoks began squeaking among themselves, pointing and gesticulating.

Threepio spoke to the one who appeared to be the leader. "Chree breeb a shurr du."

"Bloh wreee dbleeop weeschhreee!" answered the fuzzy beast.

"Du wee sheess?"

"Reeop glwah wrrripsh."

"Shreee?"

Suddenly one of the Ewoks dropped his spear with a little gasp and prostrated himself before the shiny droid. In another moment, all the Ewoks followed suit. Threepio looked at his friends with a slightly embarrassed shrug.

Chewie let out a puzzled bark. Artoo whirred speculatively. Luke and Han regarded the battalion of kowtowing Ewoks in wonder.

Then, at some invisible signal from one of their group, the small creatures began to chant in unison: "Eekee whoh, eekee whoh, Rheakee rheekee whoh..."

Han looked at Threepio with total disbelief. "What'd you *say* to them?"

"'Hello,' I think," Threepio replied almost apologetically. He hastened to add, "I could be mistaken, they're using a very primitive dialect...I believe they think I'm some sort of god."

Chewbacca and Artoo thought that was very funny. They spent several seconds hysterically barking and whistling before they finally managed to quiet down. Chewbacca had to wipe a tear from his eye.

Han just shook his head with a galaxy-weary look of patience. "Well how about using your divine influence to get us out of this?" he suggested solicitously.

Threepio pulled himself up to his full height, and spoke with unrelenting decorum. "I beg your pardon, Captain Solo, but that wouldn't be proper."

"Proper!?" Solo roared. He always knew this pompous droid was going to go too far with him one day— and this might well be the day.

"It's against my programming to impersonate a deity," he replied to Solo, as if nothing so obvious needed explanation.

Han moved threateningly toward the protocol droid, his fingers itching to pull a plug. "Listen, you pile of bolts, if you don't—" He got no farther, as fifteen Ewok spears were thrust menacingly in his face. "Just kidding," he smiled affably.

The procession of Ewoks wound its way slowly into the ever-darkening forest—tiny, somber creatures, inching through a giant's maze. The sun had nearly set, now, and the long criss-crossing shadows made the cavernous domain even more imposing than before. Yet the Ewoks seemed well at home, turning down each dense corridor of vines with precision.

On their shoulders they carried their four prisoners—Han, Chewbacca, Luke, Artoo—tied to long poles, wrapped around and around with vines, immobilizing them as if they were wriggling larvae in coarse, leafy cocoons.

Behind the captives, Threepio, borne on a litter—rough-hewn of branches in the shape of a chair—was carried high upon the shoulders of the lowly Ewoks. Like a royal potentate, he perused the mighty forest through which they carried him—the magnificent lavender sunset glowing between the vinery, the exotic flowers starting to close, the ageless trees, the glistening ferns—and knew that no one before him had ever appreciated these things in just precisely the manner he was now. No one else had his sensors, his circuits, his programs, his memory banks—and so in some real way, he *was* the creator of this little universe, its images, and colors.

And it was good.

6

THE starry sky seemed very near the treetops to Luke as he and his friends were carried into the Ewok village. He wasn't even aware it was a village at first—the tiny orange sparks of light in the distance he thought initially to be stars. This was particularly true when—dangling on his back, strapped to the pole as he was—the fiery bright points flickered directly above him, between the trees.

But then he found himself being hoisted up intricate stairways and hidden ramps *around* the immense trunks; and gradually, the higher they went, the bigger and cracklier the lights became. When the group was hundreds of feet up in the trees, Luke finally realized the lights were bonfires—*among* the treetops.

They were finally taken out onto a rickety wooden walkway, far too far off the ground to be able to see anything below them but the abysmal drop. For one bleak moment Luke was afraid they were simply going to be pitched over the brink to test their knowledge of forest lore. But the Ewoks had something else in mind.

The narrow platform ended midway between two trees. The first creature in line grabbed hold of a long vine and swung across to the far trunk—which Luke could see, by twisting his head around, had a large cavelike opening carved into its titanic surface. Vines were quickly tossed back and forth across the chasm, until soon a kind of lattice was constructed—and Luke found himself being pulled across it, on his back, still tied to the wooden poles. He looked down once, into nothingness. It was an unwelcome sensation.

On the other side they rested on a shaky, narrow platform until everyone was across. Then the diminutive monkey-bears dismantled the webbing of vines and proceeded into the tree with their captives. It was totally black inside, but Luke had the impression it was more of a tunnel through the wood than an actual cavern. The impression of dense, solid walls was everywhere, like a burrow in a mountain. When they emerged, fifty yards beyond, they were in the village square.

It was a series of wooden platforms, planks, and walkways connecting an extensive cluster of enormous trees. Supported by this scaffolding was a village of huts, constructed of an odd combination of stiffened leather, daub and wattle, thatched roofs, mud floors. Small campfires burned before many of the huts—the sparks were caught by an elaborate system of hanging vines, which funneled them to a smothering point. And everywhere, were hundreds of Ewoks.

Cooks, tanners, guards, grandfathers. Mother Ewoks gathered up squealing babies at the sight of the prisoners and scurried into their huts or pointed or murmured. Dinner smoke filled the air; children played games; minstrels played strange, resonant music on hollow logs, windy reeds.

There was vast blackness below, vaster still, above; but here in this tiny village suspended between the two, Luke felt warmth and light, and special peace.

The entourage of captors and captives stopped before the largest hut. Luke, Chewie, and Artoo were leaned, on their poles, against a nearby tree. Han was tied to a spit, and balanced above a pile of kindling that looked suspiciously like a barbecue pit. Dozens of Ewoks gathered around, chattering curiously in animated squeals.

Teebo emerged from the large structure. He was slightly bigger than most of the others, and undeniably fiercer. His fur was a pattern of light and dark gray stripes. Instead of the usual leathery hood, he wore a horned animal half-skull atop his head, which he'd further adorned with feathers. He carried a stone hatchet, and even for someone as small as an Ewok, he walked with a definite swagger.

He examined the group cursorily, then seemed to make some kind of pronouncement. At that, a member of the hunting party stepped forward—Paploo, the mantled Ewok who seemed to have taken a more protective view toward the prisoners.

Teebo conferred with Paploo for a short time. The discussion soon turned into a heated disagreement, however, with Paploo apparently taking the Rebels' side, and Teebo seemingly dismissing whatever considerations arose. The rest of the tribe stood around watching the debate with great interest, occasionally shouting comments or squeaking excitedly.

Threepio, whose litter/throne had been set down in a place of honor near the stake to which Solo was tied, followed the ongoing argument with rapt fascination. He began to translate once or twice for Luke and the others—but stopped after only a few words, since the debaters were talking so fast, he didn't want to lose the gist of what was being said. Consequently, he didn't transmit any more information than the names of the Ewoks involved.

Han looked over at Luke with a dubious frown. "I don't like the looks of this."

Chewie growled his wholehearted agreement.

Suddenly Logray exited from the large hut, silencing everyone with his presence. Shorter than Teebo, he was nonetheless clearly the object of greater general respect. He, too, wore a half-skull on his head—some kind of great bird skull, a single feather tied to its crest. His fur was striped tan, though, and his face wise. He carried no weapon; only a pouch at his side, and a staff topped by the spine of a once-powerful enemy.

One by one, he carefully appraised the captives, smelling Han, testing the fabric of Luke's clothing between his fingers. Teebo and Paploo babbled their opposing points of view at him, but he seemed supremely uninterested, so they soon stopped.

When Logray came to Chewbacca, he became fascinated, and poked at the Wookiee with his staff of bones. Chewie took exception to this, though: he growled dangerously at the tiny bear-man. Logray needed no further coaching and did a quick back-step—at the same time reaching into his pouch and sprinkling some herbs in Chewie's direction.

"Careful, Chewie," Han cautioned from across the square. "He must be the head honcho."

"No," Threepio corrected, "actually I believe he's their Medicine Man."

Luke was about to intervene, then decided to wait. It would be better if this serious little community came to its own conclusions about them, in its own way. The Ewoks seemed curiously grounded for a people so airborne.

Logray wandered over to examine Artoo-Detoo, a most wondrous creature. He sniffed, tapped, and stroked the droid's metal shell, then scrunched up his face in a look of consternation. After a few moments of thought, he ordered the small robot cut down.

The crowd murmured excitedly and backed off a few feet. Artoo's vine binders were slashed by two knife-wielding guards, causing the droid to slide down his pole and crash unceremoniously to the ground.

The guards set him upright. Artoo was instantly furious. He zeroed in on Teebo as the source of his ignominy, and beeping a blue streak, began to chase the terrified Ewok in circles. The crowd roared—some cheering on Teebo, some squeaking encouragement to the deranged droid.

Finally Artoo got close enought to Teebo to zing him with an electric charge. The shocked Ewok jumped into the air, squealed raucously, and ran away as fast as his stubby little legs could carry him. Wicket slipped surreptitiously into the big hut, as the onlookers screeched their indignation or delight.

Threepio was incensed. "Artoo, stop that! You're only going to make matters worse."

Artoo scooted over directly in front of the golden droid, and began beeping a vehement tirade. "Wreee op doo rhee vrrr gk gdk dk whoo dop dhop vree doo dweet..."

This outburst miffed Threepio substantially. With a haughty tilt he sat up straight in his throne. "That's no way to speak to someone in my position."

Luke was afraid the situation was well on its way to getting out of control. He called with the barest hint of impatience to his faithful droid. "Threepio, I think it's time you spoke on our behalf."

Threepio—rather ungraciously, actually—turned to the assemblage of fuzzy creatures and made a short speech, pointing from time to time to his friends tied to the stakes.

Logray became visibly upset by this. He waved his staff, stamped his feet, shrieked at the golden droid for a full minute. At the conclusion of his statement, he nodded to several attentive fellows, who nodded back and began filling the pit under Han with firewood.

"Well, what did he say?" Han shouted with some concern.

Threepio wilted with chagrin. "I'm rather embarrassed, Captain Solo, but it appears you are to be the main course at a banquet in my honor. He is quite offended that I should suggest otherwise."

Before another word could be said, log-drums began

beating in ominous syncopation. As one, all the furry heads turned toward the mouth of the large hut. Out of it came Wicket; and behind him, Chief Chirpa.

Chirpa was gray of fur, strong of will. On his head he bore a garland woven of leaves, teeth, and the horns of great animals he'd bested in the hunt. In his right hand he carried a staff fashioned from the longbone of a flying reptile; in his left he held an iguana, who was his pet and advisor.

He surveyed the scene in the square at a glance, then turned to wait for the guest who was only now emerging from the large hut behind him.

The guest was the beautiful young Princess of Alderaan.

"Leia!" Luke and Han shouted together.

"Rahrhah!"

"Boo dEEdwee!"

"Your Highness!"

With a gasp she rushed toward her friends, but a phalanx of Ewoks blocked her way with spears. She turned to Chief Chirpa, then to her robot interpreter.

"Threepio, tell them these are my friends. They must be set free."

Threepio looked at Chirpa and Logray. "Eep sqee rheeow," he said with much civility. "Sqeeow roah meep meeb eerah."

Chirpa and Logray shook their heads with a motion that was unequivocably negative. Logray chattered an order at his helpers, who resumed vigorously piling wood under Solo.

Han exchanged helpless looks with Leia. "Somehow I have a feeling that didn't do us much good."

"Luke, what can we do?" Leia urged. She hadn't expected this at all. She'd expected a guide back to her ship, or at worst a short supper and lodging for the night. She definitely didn't understand these creatures. "Luke?" she questioned.

Han was about to offer a suggestion when he paused, briefly taken aback by Leia's sudden intense faith in

Luke. It was something he hadn't really noted before; he merely noted it now.

Before he could speak up with his plan, though, Luke chimed in. "Threepio, tell them if they don't do as you wish, you'll become angry and use your magic."

"But Master Luke, what magic?" the droid protested. "I couldn't—"

"Tell them!" Luke ordered, uncharacteristically raising his voice. There were times when Threepio could test even the patience of a Jedi.

The interpreter-droid turned to the large audience, and spoke with great dignity. "Eemeeblee screesh oahr aish sh sheestee meep eep eep."

The Ewoks seemed greatly disturbed by this proclamation. They all backed up several steps, except for Logray, who took two steps forward. He shouted something at Threepio—something that sounded very in the nature of a challenge.

Luke closed his eyes with absolute concentration. Threepio began rattling on in a terribly unsettled manner, as if he'd been caught falsifying his own program. "They don't believe me, Master Luke, just as I told you..."

Luke wasn't listening to the droid, though; he was visualizing him. Seeing him sitting shiny and golden on his throne of twigs, nodding this way and that, prattling on about the most inconsequential of matters, sitting there in the black void of Luke's consciousness ...and slowly beginning to rise.

Slowly, Threepio began to rise.

At first, he didn't notice; at first, nobody did. Threepio just went right on talking, as his entire litter steadily elevated off the ground. "...told you, I told you, I told you they wouldn't. I don't know why you—wha—wait a minute...what's happening here?..."

Threepio and the Ewoks all realized what was happening at just about the same moment. The Ewoks silently fell back in terror from the floating throne. Threepio now began to spin, as if he were on a revolving stool. Graceful, majestic spinning.

"Help," he whispered. "Artoo, help me."

Chief Chirpa shouted orders to his cowering minions. Quickly they ran forward and released the bound prisoners. Leia, Han, and Luke enfolded each other in a long, powerful embrace. It seemed, to all of them, a strange setting in which to gain the first victory of this campaign against the Empire.

Luke was aware of a plaintive beeping behind him, and turned to see Artoo staring up at a still-spinning Threepio. Luke lowered the golden droid slowly to the ground.

"Thanks, Threepio," the young Jedi patted him gratefully on the shoulder.

Threepio, still a bit shaken, stood with a wobbly, amazed smile. "Why—why—I didn't know I had it in me."

The hut of Chief Chirpa was large, by Ewok standards—though Chewbacca, sitting cross-legged, nearly scraped the ceiling with his head. The Wookiee hunched along one side of the dwelling with his Rebel comrades, while the Chief and ten Elders sat on the other side facing them. In the center, between the two groups, a small fire warmed the night air, casting ephemeral shadows on the earthen walls.

Outside, the entire village awaited the decisions this council would arrive at. It was a pensive, clear night, charged with high moment. Though it was quite late, not an Ewok slept.

Inside, Threepio was speaking. Positive and negative feedback loops had already substantially increased his fluency in this squeaky language; he was now in the midst of an animated history of the Galactic Civil War—replete with pantomime, elocution, explosive sound effects, and editorial commentary. He even mimicked an Imperial walker at one point.

The Ewok Elders listened carefully, occasionally murmuring comments to each other. It was a fascinating story, and they were thoroughly absorbed—at times, horrified; at times, outraged. Logray conferred with

Chief Chirpa once or twice, and several times asked Threepio questions, to which the golden droid responded quite movingly—once Artoo even whistled, probably for emphasis.

In the end, though, after a rather brief discussion among the Elders, the Chief shook his head negatively, with an expression of rueful dissatisfaction. He spoke finally to Threepio, and Threepio interpreted for his friends.

"Chief Chirpa says it's a very moving story," the droid explained. "But it really has nothing to do with Ewoks."

A deep and pressing silence filled the small chamber. Only the fire softly crackled its bright but darkling soliloquy.

It was finally Solo—of all people—who opened his mouth to speak for the group. For the Alliance.

"Tell them this, Goldenrod—" he smiled at the droid, with conscious affection for the first time. "Tell them it's hard to translate a rebellion, so maybe a translator shouldn't tell the story. So *I'll* tell 'em.

"They shouldn't help us 'cause we're asking 'em to. They shouldn't even help us 'cause it's in their own interest to—even though it *is*, you know—just for one example, the Empire's tappin' a *lot* of energy out of this moon to generate its deflector shield, and that's a lot of energy you guys are gonna be *without* come winter, and I mean you're gonna be hurtin'…but never mind that. Tell 'em, Threepio."

Threepio told them. Han went on.

"But that's not why they should help us. That's why *I* used to do stuff, because it was in my interest. But not anymore. Well, not so much, anyway. Mostly I do things for my *friends*, now—'cause what else is so important? Money? Power? Jabba had that, and you know what happened to him. Okay, okay, the point is—your friends are…your *friends*. You know?"

This was one of the most inarticulate pleas Leia had ever heard, but it made her eyes fill with tears. The

Ewoks, on the other hand, remained silent, impassive. Teebo and the stoic little fellow named Paploo traded a few muttered words; the rest were motionless, their expressions unreadable.

After another protracted pause, Luke cleared his throat. "I realize this concept may be abstract—may be difficult to draw these connections," he started slowly, "but it's terribly important for the entire galaxy, for our Rebel force to destroy the Imperial presence here on Endor. Look up, there, through the smoke hole in the roof. Just through that tiny hole, you can count a hundred stars. In the whole sky there are millions, and billions more you can't even see. And they all have planets, and moons, and happy people just like you. And the Empire is destroying all that. You can...you could get dizzy just lying on your back and staring up at all the starshine. You could almost...explode, it's so beautiful sometimes. And you're part of the beauty, it's all part of the same Force. And the Empire is trying to turn out the lights."

It took a while for Threepio to finish translating this—he wanted to get all the words just right. When he did eventually stop talking, there was an extensive squeaking among the Elders, rising and falling in volume, ceasing and then resuming again.

Leia knew what Luke was trying to say, but she feared greatly that the Ewoks wouldn't see the connection. It was connected intimately, though, if she could only bridge the gap for them. She thought of her experience in the forest earlier—her sense of oneness with the trees, whose outstretched limbs seemed to touch the very stars; the stars, whose light filtered down like cascading magic. She felt the power of the magic within her, and it resonated around the hut, from being to being, flowing through her again, making her stronger, still; until she felt one with these Ewoks, nearly—felt as if she understood them, knew them; conspired with them, in the primary sense of the word: they breathed together.

The debate wound down, leaving finally another quiet moment in the hut. Leia's respirations quieted, too, in resonance; and with an air of confident serenity, she made her appeal to the council.

"Do it because of the trees," she said.

That's all she said. Everyone expected more, but there was no more; only this short, oblique outburst.

Wicket had been observing these proceedings with increasing concern, from the sidelines. On several occasions it was apparent he was restraining himself with great difficulty from entering the council's discourse— but now he jumped to his feet, paced the width of the hut several times, finally faced the Elders, and began his own impassioned speech.

"Eep eep, meep eek squee..."

Threepio translated for his friends: "Honorable Elders, we have this night received a perilous, wondrous gift. The gift of freedom. This golden god..."—here Threepio paused in his translation just long enough to savor the moment; then went on—"...This golden god, whose return to us has been prophesied since the First Tree, tells us now he will not be our Master, tells us we are free to choose as we will—that we *must* choose; as all living things must choose their own destiny. He has come, Honorable Elders, and he will go; no longer may we be slaves to his divine guidance. We are free.

"Yet how must we comport ourselves? Is an Ewok's love of the wood any less because he can leave it? No— his love is more, because he can leave it, yet he stays. So is it with the voice of the Golden One: we can close our eyes; yet we listen.

"His friends tell us of a Force, a great living spirit, of which we are all part, even as the leaves are things separate yet part of the tree. We know this spirit, Honorable Elders, though we call it not the Force. The friends of the Golden One tell us this Force is in great jeopardy, here and everywhere. When the fire reaches the forest, who is safe? Not even the Great Tree of which all things are part; nor its leaves, nor its roots, nor its birds. All are in peril, forever and ever.

"It is a brave thing to confront such a fire, Honorable Elders. Many will die, that the forest lives on.

"But the Ewoks are brave."

The little bear-creature fixed his gaze on the others in the hut. Not a word was spoken; nonetheless, the communication was intense. After a minute like this, he concluded his statement.

"Honorable Elders, we must aid this noble party not less for the trees, but more for the sake of the *leaves* on the trees. These Rebels are like the Ewoks, who are like the leaves. Battered by the wind, eaten without thought by the tumult of locusts that inhabit the world— yet do we throw ourselves on smoldering fires, that another may know the warmth of light; yet do we make a soft bed of ourselves, that another may know rest; yet do we swirl in the wind that assails us, to send the fear of chaos into the hearts of our enemies; yet do we change color, even as the season calls upon us to change. So must we help our Leafbrothers, these Rebels—for so has come a season of change upon us."

He stood, still, before them, the small fire dancing in his eye. For a timeless moment, all the world seemed still.

The Elders were moved. Without saying another word, they nodded in agreement. Perhaps they were telepathic.

In any case, Chief Chirpa stood and, without preface, made a brief pronouncement.

All at once drums began to beat throughout the entire village. The Elders jumped up—no longer at all so serious—and ran across the tent to hug the Rebels. Teebo even began to hug Artoo, but thought better of it as the little droid backed off with a low warning whistle. Teebo scurried over to hop playfully on the Wookiee's back instead.

Han smiled uncertainly. "What's going on?"

"I'm not sure," Leia answered out the side of her mouth, "but it doesn't look too bad."

Luke, like the others, was sharing the joyous occasion—whatever it meant—with a pleasant smile and diffuse good will, when suddenly a dark cloud filled his heart, hovered there, nestled a clammy chill into the corners of his soul. He wiped its traces from his visage, made his face a mask. Nobody noticed.

Threepio finally nodded his understanding to Wicket, who was explaining the situation to him. He turned, with an expansive gesture, to the Rebels. "We are now part of the tribe."

"Just what I've always wanted," said Solo.

Threepio continued talking to the others, trying to ignore the sarcastic Star Captain. "The Chief has vowed to help us in any way to rid their land of the evil ones."

"Well, short help is better than no help, I always say," Solo chuckled.

Threepio was once again rapidly overheating his circuits toward the Corellian ingrate. "Teebo says his chief scouts, Wicket and Paploo, will show us the fastest way to the shield generator."

"Tell him thanks, Goldenrod." He just loved irking Threepio. He couldn't help himself.

Chewie let out a righteous bark, happy to be on the move again. One of the Ewoks thought he was asking for food, though, and brought the Wookiee a large slab of meat. Chewbacca didn't refuse. He downed the meat in a single gulp, as several Ewoks gathered, watching in amazement. They were so incredulous at this feat, in fact, they began giggling furiously; and the laughter was so infectious, it started the Wookiee chortling. His gruff guffaws were *really* hilarious to the chuckling Ewoks, so—as was their custom—they jumped on him in a frenzy of tickling, which he returned threefold, until they all lay in a puddle, quite exhausted. Chewie wiped his eyes and grabbed another piece of meat, which he gnawed at a more leisurely pace.

Solo, meanwhile, began organizing the expedition. "How far is it? We'll need some fresh supplies. There's not much time, you know. Give me some of that, Chewie..."

Chewie snarled.

Luke drifted to the back of the hut and then slipped

outside during the commotion. Out in the square, a great party was going on—dancing, squealing, tickling—but Luke avoided this, too. He wandered away from the bonfires, away from the gaiety, to a secluded walkway on the dark side of a colossal tree.

Leia followed him.

The sounds of the forest filled the soft night air, here. Crickets, skittering rodents, desolate breezes, anguished owls. The perfumes were a mixture of night-blooming jasmine, and pine; the harmonies were strictly ethereal. The sky was crystal black.

Luke stared at the brightest star in the heavens. It looked to be fired from deep within its core by raging elemental vapors. It was the Death Star.

He couldn't take his eyes from it. Leia found him like that.

"What's wrong?" she whispered.

He smiled wearily. "Everything, I'm afraid. Or nothing, maybe. Maybe things are finally going to be as they were meant to be."

He felt the presence of Darth Vader very near.

Leia took his hand. She felt so close to Luke, yet...she couldn't say how. He seemed so lost now, so alone. So distant. She almost couldn't feel his hand in hers. "What is it, Luke?"

He looked down at their intertwined fingers. "Leia...do you remember your mother? Your real mother?"

The question took her totally by surprise. She'd always felt so close to her adopted parents, it was as if they *were* her real parents. She almost never thought of her *real* mother—that was like a dream.

Yet now Luke's question made her start. Flashes from her infancy assaulted her—distorted visions of running...a beautiful woman...hiding in a trunk. The fragments suddenly threatened to flood her with emotion.

"Yes," she said, pausing to regain her composure. "Just a little bit. She died when I was very young."

"What do you remember?" he pressed. "Tell me."

"Just feelings, really...images." She wanted to let it slide, it was so out of the blue, so far from her immediate concerns...but somehow so loud inside, all of a sudden.

"Tell me," Luke repeated.

She felt surprised by his insistence, but decided to follow him with it, at least for the time being. She trusted him, even when he frightened her. "She was very beautiful," Leia remembered aloud. "Gentle and kind—but sad." She looked deeply into his eyes, seeking his intentions. "Why are you asking me this?"

He turned away, peering back up at the Death Star, as if he'd been on the verge of opening up; then something scared him, and he pulled it all in once more. "I have no memory of my mother," he claimed. "I never knew her."

"Luke, tell me what's troubling you." She wanted to help, she knew she could help.

He stared at her a long moment, estimating her abilities, gauging her need to know, her desire to know. She was strong. He felt it, unwaveringly. He could depend on her. They all could. "Vader is here...now. On this moon."

She felt a chill, like a physical sensation, as if her blood had actually congealed. "How do you know?"

"I can feel his presence. He's come for me."

"But how could he know we were here? Was it the code, did we leave out some password?" She knew it was none of these things.

"No, it's me. He can feel it when I'm near." He held her by the shoulders. He wanted to tell her everything, but now as he tried, his will was starting to fail. "I must leave you, Leia. As long as I'm here, I endanger the whole group and our mission here." His hands trembled. "I have to face Vader."

Leia was fast becoming distraught, confused. Intimations were rushing at her like wild owls out of the night, their wings brushing her cheek, their talons catching her hair, their harsh whispers thrilling her ear: "Who? Who? Who?"

She shook her head hard. "I don't understand, Luke. What do you mean, you have to face Vader?"

He pulled her to him, his manner suddenly gentle; abidingly calm. To say it, just to say it, in some basic way released him. "He's my father, Leia."

"Your father!?" She couldn't believe it; yet of course it was true.

He held her steady, to be a rock for her. "Leia, I've found something else out. It's not going to be easy for you to hear it, but you have to. You have to know before I leave here because I might not be back. And if I don't make it, you're the only hope for the Alliance."

She looked away, she shook her head, she wouldn't look at him. It was terribly disturbing, what Luke was saying, though she couldn't imagine why. It was non-sense, of course; *that* was why. To call her the only hope for the Alliance if he should die—why, it was absurd. Absurd to think of Luke dying, and to think of her being the only hope.

Both thoughts were out of the question. She moved away from him, to deny his words; at least to give them distance, to let her breathe. Flashes of her mother came again, in this breathing space. Parting embraces, flesh torn from flesh...

"Don't talk that way, Luke. You have to survive. I do what I can—we all do—but I'm of no importance. Without you...I can do nothing. It's you, Luke. I've seen it. You have a power I don't understand...and could never have."

"You're wrong, Leia." He held her at arm's length. "You have that power, too. The Force is strong in you. In time you'll learn to use it as I have."

She shook her head. She couldn't hear this. He was lying. She had no power, the power was elsewhere, she could only help and succor and support. What was he saying? Was it possible?

He brought her closer still, held her face in his hands.

He looked so tender now, so giving. Was he giving her the power? Could she truly hold it? What was he saying? "Luke, what's come over you?"

"Leia, the Force is strong in my family. My father has it, I have it, and...my sister has it."

Leia stared full into his eyes again. Darkness whirled there. And truth. What she saw frightened her...but now, this time, she didn't draw away. She stood close to him. She started to understand.

"Yes," he whispered, seeing her comprehension. "Yes. It's you, Leia." He held her in his arms.

Leia closed her eyes tightly against his words, against her tears. To no avail. It all washed over her, now, and through her. "I know," she nodded. Openly she wept.

"Then you know I must go to him."

She stood back, her face hot, her mind swimming in a storm. "No, Luke, no. Run away, far away. If he can feel your presence, go away from this place." She held his hands, put her cheek on his chest. "I wish I could go with you."

He stroked the back of her head. "No, you don't. You've never faltered. When Han and I and the others have doubted, you've always been strong. You've never turned away from your responsibility. I can't say the same." He thought of his premature flight from Dagobah, racing to risk everything before his training had been completed, almost destroying everything because of it. He looked down at the black, mechanical hand he had to show for it. How much more would be lost to his weakness? "Well," he choked, "now we're both going to fulfill our destinies."

"Luke, why? Why must you confront him?"

He thought of all the reasons—to win, to lose, to join, to struggle, to kill, to weep, to walk away, to accuse, to ask why, to forgive, to not forgive, to die—but knew, in the end, there was only one reason, now and always. Only one reason that could ever matter. "There's good in him, I've felt it. He won't give me over to the Emperor. I can save him, I can turn him back to the good side." His eyes became wild for just a moment, torn by doubts and passions. "I have to try, Leia. He's our father."

They held each other close. Tears streamed silently down her face.

"Goodbye, dear sister—lost, and found. Goodbye, sweet, sweet Leia."

She cried openly, now—they both did—as Luke held her away and moved slowly back along the planking. He disappeared into the darkness of the tree-cave that led out of the village.

Leia watched him go, quietly weeping. She gave free vent to her feelings, did not try to stop the tears—tried, instead, to feel them, to feel the source they came from, the path they took, the murky corners they cleansed.

Memories poured through her, now, clues, suspicions, half-heard mutterings when they'd thought she was asleep. Luke, her brother! And Vader, her father. This was too much to assimilate all at once, it was information overload.

She was crying and trembling and whimpering all at once, when suddenly Han stepped up and embraced her from behind. He'd gone looking for her, and heard her voice, and came around just in time to see Luke leaving—but only now, when Leia jumped at his touch and he turned her around, did he realize she was sobbing.

His quizzical smile turned to concern, tempered by the heart-fear of the would-be lover. "Hey, what's going on here?"

She stifled her sobs, wiped her eyes. "It's nothing, Han. I just want to be alone for a while."

She was hiding something, that much was plain, and that much was unacceptable. "It's not nothing!" he said angrily. "I want to know what's going on. Now you tell me what it is." He shook her. He'd never felt like this before. He wanted to know, but he didn't want to know what he thought he knew. It made him sick at heart to think of Leia...with Luke...he couldn't even bring himself to imagine what it was he didn't want to imagine.

He'd never been out of control like this, he didn't like it, he couldn't stop it. He realized he was still shaking her, and stopped.

"I can't, Han..." Her lip began to tremble again.

"You can't! You can't tell *me*? I thought we were closer than that, but I guess I was wrong. Maybe you'd rather tell Luke. Sometimes I—"

"Oh, Han!" she cried, and burst into tears once more. She buried herself in his embrace.

His anger turned slowly to confusion and dismay, as he found himself wrapping his arms around her, caressing her shoulders, comforting her. "I'm sorry," he whispered into her hair. "I'm sorry." He didn't understand, not an iota—didn't understand her, or himself, or his topsy-turvy feelings, or women, or the universe. All he knew was that he'd just been furious, and now he was affectionate, protective, tender. Made no sense.

"Please...just hold me," she whispered. She didn't want to talk. She just wanted to be held.

He just held her.

Morning mist rose off dewy vegetation as the sun broke the horizon over Endor. The lush foliage of the forest's edge had a moist, green odor; in that dawning moment the world was silent, as if holding its breath.

In violent contrast, the Imperial landing platform squatted over the ground. Harsh, metallic, octagonal, it seemed to cut like an insult into the verdant beauty of the place. The bushes at its perimeter were singed black from repeated shuttle landings; the flora beyond that was wilting—dying from refuse disposal, trampling feet, chemical exhaust fumes. Like a blight was this outpost.

Uniformed troops walked continuously on the platform and in the area—loading, unloading, surveilling, guarding. Imperial walkers were parked off to one side—square, armored, two-legged war machines, big enough for a squad of soldiers to stand inside, firing laser cannon in all directions. An Imperial shuttle took off for the Death Star, with a roar that made the trees cringe. Another walker emerged from the timber on the far side of the platform, returning from a patrol mission. Step by lumbering step, it approached the loading dock.

Darth Vader stood at the rail of the lower deck, staring mutely into the depths of the lovely forest. Soon. It was coming soon; he could feel it. Like a drum getting louder, his destiny approached. Dread was all around, but fear like this excited him, so he let it bubble quietly within. Dread was a tonic, it heightened his senses, honed a raw edge to his passions. Closer, it came.

Victory, too he sensed. Mastery. But laced with something else... what was it? He couldn't see it, quite. Always in motion, the future; difficult to see. Its apparitions tantalized him, swirling specters, always changing. Smoky was his future, thunderous with conquest and destruction.

Very close, now. Almost here.

He purred, in the pit of his throat, like a wild cat smelling game on the air.

Almost here.

The Imperial walker docked at the opposite end of the deck, and opened its doors. A phalanx of stormtroopers marched out in tight circular formation. They lock-stepped toward Vader.

He turned around to face the oncoming troopers, his breathing even, his black robes hanging still in the windless morning. The stormtroopers stopped when they reached him, and at a word from their captain, parted to reveal a bound prisoner in their midst. It was Luke Skywalker.

The young Jedi gazed at Vader with complete calm, with many layers of vision.

The stormtrooper captain spoke to Lord Vader. "This is the Rebel that surrendered to us. Although he denies it, I believe there may be more of them, and I request permission to conduct a wider search of the area." He extended his hand to the Dark Lord; in it, he held Luke's lightsaber. "He was armed only with this."

Vader looked at the lightsaber a moment, then slowly took it from the captain's hand. "Leave us. Conduct your search, and bring his companions to me."

The officer and his troops withdrew back to the walker.

Luke and Vader were left standing alone facing each other, in the emerald tranquillity of the ageless forest. The mist was beginning to burn off. Long day ahead.

 7

"SO," the Dark Lord rumbled. "You have come to me."

"And you to me."

"The Emperor is expecting you. He believes you will turn to the dark side."

"I know...Father." It was a momentous act for Luke—to address his father, as his father. But he'd done it, now, and kept himself under control, and the moment was past. It was done. He felt stronger for it. He felt potent.

"So, you have finally accepted the truth," Vader gloated.

"I have accepted the truth that you were once Anakin Skywalker, my father."

"That name no longer has meaning for me." It was a name from long ago. A different life, a different universe. Could he truly once have been that man?

"It is the name of your true self," Luke's gaze bore steadily down on the cloaked figure. "You have only forgotten. I know there is good in you. The Emperor hasn't driven it fully away." He molded with his voice,

125

tried to form the potential reality with the strength of his belief. "That's why you could not destroy me. That's why you won't take me to your Emperor now."

Vader seemed almost to smile through his mask at his son's use of Jedi voice-manipulation. He looked down at the lightsaber the captain had given him— Luke's lightsaber. So the boy was truly a Jedi now. A man grown. He held the lightsaber up. "You have constructed another."

"This one is mine," Luke said quietly. "I no longer use yours."

Vader ignited the blade, examined its humming, brilliant light, like an admiring craftsman. "Your skills are complete. Indeed, you are as powerful as the Emperor has foreseen."

They stood there for a moment, the lightsaber between them. Sparks dove in and out of the cutting edge: photons pushed to the brink by the energy pulsing between these two warriors.

"Come with me, Father."

Vader shook his head. "Ben once thought as you do—"

"Don't blame Ben for your fall—" Luke took a step closer, then stopped.

Vader did not move. "You don't know the power of the dark side. I must obey my master."

"I will not turn—you will be forced to destroy me."

"If that is your destiny." This was not his wish, but the boy was strong—if it came, at last, to blows, yes, he would destroy Luke. He could no longer afford to hold back, as he once had.

"Search your feelings, Father. You can't do this. I feel the conflict within you. Let go of your hate."

But Vader hated no one; he only lusted too blindly. "Someone has filled your mind with foolish ideas, young one. The Emperor will show you the true nature of the Force. *He* is your master, now."

Vader signaled to a squad of distant stormtroopers as he extinguished Luke's lightsaber. The guards approached. Luke and the Dark Lord faced one another for a long, searching moment. Vader spoke just before the guards arrived.

"It is too late for me, Son."

"Then my father is truly dead," answered Luke. So what was to stop him from killing the Evil One who stood before him now? he wondered.

Nothing, perhaps.

The vast Rebel fleet hung poised in space, ready to strike. It was hundreds of light-years from the Death Star—but in hyperspace, all time was a moment, and the deadliness of an attack was measured not in distance but in precision.

Ships changed in formation from corner to side, creating a faceted diamond shape to the armada—as if, like a cobra, the fleet was spreading its hood.

The calculations required to launch such a meticulously coordinated offensive at lightspeed made it necessary to fix on a stationary point—that is, stationary relative to the point of reentry from hyperspace. The point chosen by the Rebel command was a small, blue planet of the Sullust system. The armada was positioned around it, now, this unblinking cerulean world. It looked like the eye of the serpent.

The *Millennium Falcon* finished its rounds of the fleet's perimeter, checking final positions, then pulled into place beneath the flagship. The time had come.

Lando was at the controls of the *Falcon*. Beside him, his copilot, Nien Nunb—a jowled, mouse-eyed creature from Sullust—flipped switches, monitored readouts, and made final preparations for the jump to hyperspace.

Lando set his comlink to war channel. Last hand of the night, his deal, a table full of high rollers—his favorite kind of game. With dry mouth, he made his summary report to Ackbar on the command ship. "Admiral, we're in position. All fighters are accounted for."

Ackbar's voice crackled back over the headset. "Proceed with the countdown. All groups assume attack coordinates."

Lando turned to his copilot with a quick smile. "Don't worry, my friends are down there, they'll have that shield down on time..." He turned back to his instruments, saying under his breath: "Or this will be the shortest offensive of all time."

"Gzhung Zhgodio," the copilot commented.

"All right," Lando grunted. "Stand by, then." He patted the control panel for good luck, even though his deepest belief was that a good gambler made his own luck. Still, that's what Han's job was this time, and Han had almost never let Lando down. Just once—and that was a long time ago, in a star system far, far away.

This time was different. This time they were going to redefine luck, and call it Lando. He smiled, and patted the panel one more time...just right.

Up on the bridge of the Star Cruiser command ship, Ackbar paused, looked around at his generals: all was ready.

"Are all groups in their attack coordinates?" he asked. He knew they were.

"Affirmative, Admiral."

Ackbar gazed out his view-window meditatively at the starfield, for perhaps the last reflective moment he would ever have. He spoke finally into the comlink war channel. "All craft will begin the jump to hyperspace on my mark. May the Force be with us."

He reached forward to the signal button.

In the *Falcon*, Lando stared at the identical galactic ocean, with the same sense of grand moment; but also with foreboding. They were doing what a guerrilla force must never do: engage the enemy like a traditional army. The Imperial army, fighting the Rebellion's guerrilla war, was always losing—unless it won. The Rebels, by contrast, were always winning—unless they lost. And now, here was the most dangerous situation— the Alliance drawn into the open, to fight on the Empire's terms: if the Rebels lost this battle, they lost the war.

Suddenly the signal light flashed on the control panel: Ackbar's mark. The attack was commenced.

Lando pulled back the conversion switch and opened up the throttle. Outside the cockpit, the stars began streaking by. The streaks grew brighter, and longer, as the ships of the fleet roared, in large segments, at light-speed, keeping pace first with the very photons of the radiant stars in the vicinity, and then soaring through the warp into hyperspace itself—and disappearing in the flash of a muon.

The blue crystal planet hovered in space alone, once again; staring, unseeing, into the void.

The strike squad crouched behind a woodsy ridge overlooking the Imperial outpost. Leia viewed the area through a small electronic scanner.

Two shuttles were being off-loaded on the landing platform docking ramp. Several walkers were parked nearby. Troops stood around, helped with construction, took watch, carried supplies. The massive shield generator hummed off to the side.

Flattened down in the bushes on the ridge with the strike force were several Ewoks, including Wicket, Paploo, Teebo, and Warwick. The rest stayed lower, behind the knoll, out of sight.

Leia put down the scanner and scuttled back to the others. "The entrance is on the far side of that landing platform. This isn't going to be easy."

"Ahrck grah rahr hrowrowhr," Chewbacca agreed.

"Oh, come on, Chewie," Han gave the Wookiee a pained look. "We've gotten into more heavily guarded places than that—"

"Frowh rahgh rahrahraff vrawgh gr," Chewie countered with a dismissing gesture.

Han thought for a second. "Well, the spice vaults of Gargon, for one."

"Krahghrowf," Chewbacca shook his head.

"Of course I'm right—now if I could just remember how I did it..." Han scratched his head, poking his memory.

Suddenly Paploo began chattering away, pointing, squealing. He garbled something to Wicket.

"What's he saying, Threepio?" Leia asked.

The golden droid exchanged a few terse sentences with Paploo; then Wicket turned to Leia with a hopeful grin.

Threepio, too, now looked at the Princess. "Apparently Wicket knows about a back entrance to this installation."

Han perked up at that. "A back door? That's it! That's how we did it!"

Four Imperial scouts kept watch over the entrance to the bunker that half-emerged from the earth far to the rear of the main section of the shield generator complex. Their rocket bikes were parked nearby.

In the undergrowth beyond, the Rebel strike squad lay in wait.

"Grrr, rowf rrrhl brhnnnh," Chewbacca observed slowly.

"You're right, Chewie," Solo agreed, "with just those guards this should be easier than breaking a Bantha."

"It only takes one to sound the alarm," Leia cautioned.

Han grinned, a bit overselfconfidently. "Then we'll have to do this real quietlike. If Luke can just keep Vader off our backs, like you said he said he would, this oughta be no sweat. Just gotta hit those guards fast and quiet..."

Threepio whispered to Teebo and Paploo, explaining the problem and the objective. The Ewoks babbled giddily a moment, then Paploo jumped up and raced through the underbrush.

Leia checked the instrument on her wrist. "We're running out of time. The fleet's in hyperspace by now."

Threepio muttered a question to Teebo and received a short reply. "Oh, dear," Threepio replied, starting to rise, to look into the clearing beside the bunker.

"Stay down!" rasped Solo.

"What is it, Threepio?" Leia demanded.

"I'm afraid our furry companion has gone and done

something rash." The droid hoped *he* wasn't to be blamed for this.

"What are you talking about?" Leia's voice cut with an edge of fear.

"Oh, no. Look."

Paploo had scampered down through the bushes to where the scouts' bikes were parked. Now, with the sickening horror of inevitability, the Rebel leaders watched the little ball of fur swing his pudgy body up onto one of the bikes, and begin flipping switches at random. Before anyone could do anything, the bike's engines ignited with a rumbling roar. The four scouts looked over in surprise. Paploo grinned madly, and continued flipping switches.

Leia held her forehead. "Oh, no, no, no."

Chewie barked. Han nodded. "So much for our surprise attack."

The Imperial scouts raced toward Paploo just as the forward drive engaged, zooming the little teddy bear into the forest. He had all he could do just to hang on to the handlebar with his stubby paws. Three of the guards jumped on their own bikes, and sped off in pursuit of the hotrod Ewok. The fourth scout stayed at his post, near the door of the bunker.

Leia was delighted, if a bit incredulous.

"Not bad for a ball of fuzz," Han admired. He nodded at Chewie, and the two of them slipped down toward the bunker.

Paploo, meanwhile, was sailing through the trees, more lucky than in control. He was going at fairly low velocity for what the bike could do—but in Ewok-time, Paploo was absolutely dizzy with speed and excitement. It was terrifying; but he loved it. He would talk about this ride until the end of his life, and then his children would tell their children, and it would get faster with each generation.

For now, though, the Imperial scouts were already pulling in sight behind him. When, a moment later, they began firing laser bolts at him, he decided he'd finally had enough. As he rounded the next tree, just out of their sight, he grabbed a vine and swung up into the branches. Several seconds later the three scouts tore by underneath him, pressing their pursuit to the limit. He giggled furiously.

Back at the bunker, the last scout was undone. Subdued by Chewbacca, bound, stripped of his suit, he was being carried into the woods now by two other members of the strike team. The rest of the squad silently crouched, forming a perimeter around the entrance.

Han stood at the door, checking the stolen code against the digits on the bunker's control panel. With natural speed he punched a series of buttons on the panel. Silently, the door opened.

Leia peeked inside. No sign of life. She motioned the others, and entered the bunker. Han and Chewie followed close on her heels. Soon the entire team was huddled inside the otherwise empty steel corridor, leaving one lookout outside, dressed in the unconscious scout's uniform. Han pushed a series of buttons on the inner panel, closing the door behind them.

Leia thought briefly of Luke—she hoped he could detain Vader at least long enough to allow her to destroy this shield generator; she hoped even more dearly he could avoid such a confrontation altogether. For she feared Vader was the stronger of the two.

Furtively she led the way down the dark and low-beamed tunnel.

Vader's shuttle settled onto the docking bay of the Death Star, like a black, wingless carrion-eating bird; like a nightmare insect. Luke and the Dark Lord emerged from the snout of the beast with a small escort of stormtroopers, and walked rapidly across the cavernous main bay to the Emperor's tower elevator.

Royal guards awaited them there, flanking the shaft, bathed in a carmine glow. They opened the elevator door. Luke stepped forward.

His mind was buzzing with what to do. It was the Emperor he was being taken to, now. The Emperor!

If Luke could but focus, keep his mind clear to see what must be done—and do it.

A great noise filled his head, though, like an underground wind.

He hoped Leia deactivated the deflector shield quickly, and destroyed the Death Star—now, while all three of them were here. Before anything else happened. For the closer Luke came to the Emperor, the more *anythings* he feared *would* happen. A black storm raged inside him. He wanted to kill the Emperor, but then what? Confront Vader? What would his father do? And what if Luke faced his father first, faced him and—destroyed him. The thought was at once repugnant and compelling. Destroy Vader—and then what. For the first time, Luke had a brief murky image of himself, standing on his father's body, holding his father's blazing power, and sitting at the Emperor's right hand.

He squeezed his eyes shut against this thought, but it left a cold sweat on his brow, as if Death's hand had brushed him there and left its shallow imprint.

The elevator door opened. Luke and Vader walked out into the throne room alone, across the unlit antechamber, up the grated stairs, to stand before the throne: father and son, side by side, both dressed in black, one masked and one exposed, beneath the gaze of the malignant Emperor.

Vader bowed to his master. The Emperor motioned him to rise, though; the Dark Lord did his master's bidding.

"Welcome, young Skywalker," the Evil One smiled graciously. "I have been expecting you."

Luke stared back brazenly at the bent, hooded figure. Defiantly. The Emperor's smile grew even softer, though; even more fatherly. He looked at Luke's manacles.

"You no longer need these," he added with *noblesse oblige*—and made the slightest motion with his finger in the direction of Luke's wrists. At that, Luke's binders simply fell away, clattering noisily to the floor.

Luke looked at his own hands—free, now, to reach

out for the Emperor's throat, to crush his windpipe in an instant...

Yet the Emperor seemed gentle. Had he not just let Luke free? But he was devious, too, Luke knew. Do not be fooled by appearances, Ben had told him. The Emperor was unarmed. He could still strike. But wasn't aggression part of the dark side? Mustn't he avoid that at all costs? Or could he use darkness judiciously, and then put it away? He stared at his free hands...he could have ended it all right there—or could he? He had total freedom to choose what to do now; yet he could not choose. Choice, the double-edged sword. He could kill the Emperor, he could succumb to the Emperor's arguments. He could kill Vader...and then he could even become Vader. Again this thought laughed at him like a broken clown, until he pushed it back into a black corner of his brain.

The Emperor sat before him, smiling. The moment was convulsive with possibilities...

The moment passed. He did nothing.

"Tell me, young Skywalker," the Emperor said when he saw Luke's first struggle had taken its course. "Who has been involved in your training until now?" The smile was thin, open-mouthed, hollow.

Luke was silent. He would reveal nothing.

"Oh, I know it was Obi-Wan Kenobi at first," the wicked ruler continued, rubbing his fingers together as if trying to remember. Then pausing, his lips creased into a sneer. "Of course, we are familiar with the talent Obi-Wan Kenobi had, when it came to training Jedi." He nodded politely in Vader's direction, indicating Obi-Wan's previous star pupil. Vader stood without responding, without moving.

Luke tensed with fury at the Emperor's defamation of Ben—though, of course, to the Emperor it was praise. And he bridled even more, knowing the Emperor was so nearly right. He tried to bring his anger under control, though, for it seemed to please the malevolent dictator greatly.

Palpatine noted the emotions on Luke's face and chuckled. "So, in your early training you have followed your father's path, it would seem. But alas, Obi-Wan is now dead, I believe; his elder student, here, saw to that—" again, he made a hand motion toward Vader. "So tell me, young Skywalker—who continued your training?"

That smile, again, like a knife. Luke held silent, struggling to regain his composure.

The Emperor tapped his fingers on the arm of the throne, recalling. "There was one called...Yoda. An aged Master Jed...Ah, I see by your countenance I have hit a chord, a resonant chord indeed. Yoda, then."

Luke flashed with anger at himself, now, to have revealed so much, unwillingly, unwittingly. Anger and self-doubt. He strove to calm himself—to see all, to show nothing; only to be.

"This Yoda," the Emperor mused. "Lives he still?"

Luke focused on the emptiness of space beyond the window behind the Emperor's chair. The deep void, where nothing was. Nothing. He filled his mind with this black nothing. Opaque, save for the occasional flickering of starlight that filtered through the ether.

"Ah," cried Emperor Palpatine. "He lives not. Very good, young Skywalker, you almost hid this from me. But you could not. And you can not. Your deepest flickerings are to me apparent. Your nakedest soul. That is my first lesson to you." He beamed.

Luke wilted—but a moment. In the very faltering, he found strength. Thus had Ben and Yoda both instructed him: when you are attacked, fall. Let your opponent's power buffet you as a strong wind topples the grass. In time, he will expend himself, and you will still be upright.

The Emperor watched Luke's face with cunning. "I'm sure Yoda taught you to use the Force with great skill."

The taunt had its desired effect—Luke's face flushed, his muscles flexed.

He saw the Emperor actually lick his lips at the sight of Luke's reaction. Lick his lips and laugh from the bottom of his throat, the bottom of his soul.

Luke paused, for he saw something else, as well; something he hadn't seen before in the Emperor. Fear.

Luke saw fear in the Emperor—fear of Luke. Fear of Luke's power, fear that this power could be turned on him—on the Emperor—in the same way Vader had turned it on Obi-Wan Kenobi. Luke saw this fear in the Emperor—and he knew, now, the odds had shifted slightly. He had glimpsed the Emperor's nakedest self.

With sudden absolute calm, Luke stood upright. He stared directly into the malign ruler's hood.

Palpatine said nothing for a few moments, returning the young Jedi's gaze, assessing his strengths and weaknesses. He sat back at last, pleased with this first confrontation. "I look forward to completing your training, young Skywalker. In time, you will call *me* Master."

For the first time, Luke felt steady enough to speak. "You're gravely mistaken. You will not convert me as you did my father."

"No, my young Jedi," the Emperor leaned forward, gloating, "you will find that it is *you* who are mistaken...about a great many things."

Palpatine suddenly stood, came down from his throne, walked up very close to Luke, stared venomously into the boy's eyes. At last, Luke saw the entire face within the hood: eyes, sunken like tombs; the flesh decayed beneath skin weathered by virulent storms, lined by holocaust; the grin, a death's-grin; the breath, corrupt.

Vader extended a gloved hand toward the Emperor, holding out Luke's lightsaber. The Emperor took it with a slow sort of glee, then walked with it across the room to the huge circular view-window. The Death Star had been revolving slowly, so the Sanctuary Moon was now visible at the window's curving margin.

Palpatine looked at Endor, then back at the lightsaber in his hand. "Ah, yes, a Jedi's weapon. Much like your father's." He faced Luke directly. "By now you must know your father can never be turned from the dark side. So will it be with you."

"Never. Soon I will die, and you with me." Luke was confident of that now. He allowed himself the luxury of a boast.

The Emperor laughed, a vile laugh. "Perhaps you refer to the imminent attack of your Rebel fleet." Luke had a thick, reeling moment, then steadied himself. The Emperor went on. "I assure you, we are quite safe from your friends here."

Vader walked toward the Emperor, stood at his side, looking at Luke.

Luke felt increasingly raw. "Your overconfidence is your weakness," he challenged them.

"Your faith in your friends is yours." The Emperor began smiling; but then his mouth turned down, his voice grew angry. "Everything that has transpired has done so according to *my* design. Your friends up there on the Sanctuary Moon—they're walking into a trap. And so is your Rebel fleet!"

Luke's face twitched visibly. The Emperor saw this, and really began to foam. "It was *I* who allowed the Alliance to know the location of the shield generator. It is quite safe from your pitiful little band—an entire legion of my troops awaits them there."

Luke's eyes darted from the Emperor, to Vader, and finally to the lightsaber in the Emperor's hand. His mind quivered with alternatives; suddenly everything was out of control again. He could count on nothing but himself. And on himself, his hold was tenuous.

The Emperor kept rattling on imperiously. "I'm afraid the deflector shield will be quite operational when your fleet arrives. And that is only the beginning of my surprise—but of course I don't wish to spoil it for you."

The situation was degenerating fast, from Luke's perspective. Defeat after defeat was being piled on his head. How much could he take? And now another surprise coming? There seemed to be no end to the rank deeds Palpatine could carry out against the galaxy. Slowly, infinitesimally, Luke raised his hand in the direction of the lightsaber.

The Emperor continued. "From here, young Skywalker, you will witness the final destruction of the Alliance—and the end of your insignificant rebellion."

Luke was in torment. He raised his hand further. He realized both Palpatine and Vader were watching him. He lowered his hand, lowered his level of anger, tried to restore his previous calm, to find his center to see what it was he needed to do.

The Emperor smiled, a thin dry smile. He offered the lightsaber to Luke. "You want this, don't you? The hate is swelling in you, now. Very good, take your Jedi weapon. Use it. I am unarmed. Strike me down with it. Give in to your anger. With each passing moment you make yourself more my servant."

His rasping laughter echoed off the walls like desert wind. Vader continued staring at Luke.

Luke tried to hide his agony. "No, never." He thought desperately of Ben and Yoda. They were part of the Force, now, part of the energy that shaped it. Was it possible for them to distort the Emperor's vision by their presence? No one was infallible, Ben had told him—surely the Emperor couldn't see everything, couldn't know every future, twist every reality to suit his gluttony. *Ben*, thought Luke, *if ever I needed your guidance, it is now. Where can I take this, that it will not lead me to ruin?*

As if in answer, the Emperor leered, and put the lightsaber down on the control chair near Luke's hand. "It is unavoidable," the Emperor said quietly. "It is your destiny. You, like your father, are now...mine."

Luke had never felt so lost.

Han, Chewie, Leia, and a dozen commandos made their way down the labyrinthine corridors toward the area where the shield generator room was marked on the stolen map. Yellow lights illuminated the low rafters, casting long shadows at each intersection. At the first three turnings, all remained quiet; they saw no guard or worker.

At the fourth cross-corridor, six Imperial stormtroopers stood a wary watch.

There was no way around; the section had to be traversed. Han and Leia looked at each other and shrugged; there was nothing for it but to fight.

With pistols drawn, they barged into the entryway. Almost as if they'd been expecting an attack, the guards instantly crouched and began firing their own weapons. A barrage of laserbolts followed, ricocheting from girder to floor. Two stormtroopers were hit immediately. A third lost his gun; pinned behind a refrigerator console, he was unable to do much but stay low.

Two more stood behind a fire door, though, and blasted each commando who tried to get through. Four went down. The guards were virtually impregnable behind their vulcanized shield—but *virtually* didn't account for Wookiees.

Chewbacca rushed the door, physically dislodging it on top of the two stormtroopers. They were crushed.

Leia shot the sixth guard as he stood to draw a bead on Chewie. The trooper who'd been crouching beneath the refrigeration unit suddenly bolted, to go for help. Han raced after him a few long strides and brought him down with a flying tackle. He was out cold.

They checked themselves over, accounted for casualties. Not too bad—but it had been noisy. They'd have to hurry now, before a general alarm was set. The power center that controlled the shield generator was very near. And there would be no second chances.

The Rebel fleet broke out of hyperspace with an awesome roar. Amid glistening streamers of light, battalion after battalion emerged in formation, to fire off toward the Death Star and its Sanctuary Moon hovering brightly in the close distance. Soon the entire navy was bearing down on its target, the *Millennium Falcon* in the lead.

Lando was worried from the moment they came out

of hyperspace. He checked his screen, reversed polar-
ities, queried the computer.

The copilot was perplexed, as well. "Zhng ahzi
gngnohzh. Dzhy lyhz!"

"But how could that be?" Lando demanded. "We've
got to be able to get *some* kind of reading on the shield,
up or down." Who was conning whom on this raid?

Nien Nunb pointed at the control panel, shaking his
head. "Dzhmbd."

"Jammed? How could they be jamming us if they
don't know we're...coming."

He grimaced at the onrushing Death Star, as the
implications of what he'd just said sank in. This was
not a surprise attack, after all. It was a spider web.

He hit the switch on his comlink. "Break off the
attack! The shield's still up!"

Red Leader's voice shouted back over the head-
phones. "I get no reading, are you sure?"

"Pull up!" Lando commanded. "All craft pull up!"

He banked hard to the left, the fighters of the Red
Squad veering close on his tail.

Some didn't make it. Three flanking X-wings nicked
the invisible deflector shield, spinning out of control,
exploding in flames along the shield surface. None of
the others paused to look back.

On the Rebel Star Cruiser bridge, alarms were
screaming, lights flashing, klaxons blaring, as the mammoth space cruiser abruptly altered its momentum,
trying to change course in time to avoid collision with
the shield. Officers were running from battle stations
to navigation controls; other ships in the fleet could
be seen through the view-screens, careening wildly in
a hundred directions, some slowing, some speeding
up.

Admiral Ackbar spoke urgently but quietly into the
comlink. "Take evasive action. Green Group steer
course for Holding Sector. MG-7 Blue Group—"

A Mon Calamari controller, across the bridge, called
out to Ackbar with grave excitement. "Admiral, we have
enemy ships at Sector RT-23 and PB-4."

The large central view-screen was coming alive. It was no longer just the Death Star and the green moon behind it, floating isolated in space. Now the massive Imperial fleet could be seen flying in perfect, regimental formation, out from behind Endor in two behemoth flanking waves—heading to surround the Rebel fleet from both sides, like the pincers of a deadly scorpion.

And the shield barricaded the Alliance in front. They had nowhere to go.

Ackbar spoke desperately into the comlink. "It's a trap. Prepare for attack."

An anonymous fighter pilot's voice came back over the radio. "Fighters coming in! Here we go!"

The attack began. The battle was joined.

TIE fighters, first—they were much faster than the bulky Imperial cruisers, so they were the first to make contact with the Rebel invaders. Savage dogfights ensued, and soon the black sky was aglow with ruby explosions.

An aide approached Ackbar. "We've added power to the forward shield, Admiral."

"Good. Double power on the main battery, and—"

Suddenly the Star Cruiser was rocked by thermonuclear fireworks outside the observation window.

"Gold Wing is hit hard!" another officer shouted, stumbling up to the bridge.

"Give them cover!" Ackbar ordered. "We must have time!" He spoke again into the comlink, as yet another detonation rumbled the frigate. "All ships, stand your position. Wait for my command to return!"

It was far too late for Lando and his attack squadrons to heed that order, though. They were already way ahead of the pack, heading straight for the oncoming Imperial fleet.

Wedge Antilles, Luke's old buddy from the first campaign, led the X-wings that accompanied the *Falcon*. As they drew near the Imperial defenders, his voice came over the comlink, calm and experienced. "Lock X-foils in attack positions."

The wings split like dragonfly gossamers, poised for increased maneuvering and power.

"All wings report in," said Lando.

"Red Leader standing by," Wedge replied.

"Green Leader standing by."

"Blue Leader standing by."

"Gray Leader—"

This last transmission was interrupted by a display of pyrotechnics that completely disintegrated Gray Wing.

"Here they come," Wedge commented.

"Accelerate to attack speed," Lando ordered. "Draw fire away from our cruisers as long as possible."

"Copy, Gold Leader," Wedge responded. "We're moving to point three across the axis—"

"Two of them coming in at twenty degrees—" someone advised.

"I see them," noted Wedge. "Cut left, I'll take the leader."

"Watch yourself, Wedge, three from above."

"Yeah, I—"

"I'm on it, Red Leader."

"There's too many of them—"

"You're taking a lot of fire, back off—"

"Red Four, watch out!"

"I'm hit!"

The X-wing spun, sparking, across the starfield, out of power, into the void.

"You've picked one up, watch it!" Red Six yelled at Wedge.

"My scope's negative, where is he?"

"Red Six, a squadron of fighters has broken through—"

"They're heading for the Medical Frigate! After them!"

"Go ahead," Lando agreed. "I'm going in. There're four marks at point three five. Cover me!"

"Right behind you, Gold Leader. Red Two, Red Three, pull in—"

"Hang on, back there."

"Close up formations, Blue Group."

"Good shooting, Red Two."

"Not bad," said Lando. "I'll take out the other three..."

Calrissian steered the *Falcon* into the complete flip, as his crew fired at the Imperial fighters from the belly guns. Two were direct hits, the third a glancing blow that caused the TIE fighter to tumble into another of its own squads. The heavens were absolutely thick with them, but the *Falcon* was faster by half than anything else that flew.

Within a matter of minutes, the battlefield was a diffuse red glow, spotted with puffs of smoke, blazing fireballs, whirling spark showers, spinning debris, rumbling implosions, shafts of light, tumbling machinery, space-frozen corpses, wells of blackness, electron storms.

It was a grim and dazzling spectacle. And only beginning.

Nien Nunb made a guttural aside to Lando.

"You're right," the pilot frowned. "Only their fighters are attacking. What are those Star Destroyers waiting for?" Looked like the Emperor was trying to get the Rebels to buy some real estate he wasn't intending to sell.

"Dzhng zhng," the copilot warned, as another squadron of TIE fighters swooped down from above.

"I see 'em. We're sure in the middle of it, now." He took a second to glance at Endor, floating peacefully off to his right. "Come on, Han old buddy, don't let me down."

Han pressed the button on his wrist-unit and covered his head: the reinforced door to the main control room blew into melted pieces. The Rebel squad stormed through the gaping portal.

The stormtroopers inside seemed taken completely by surprise. A few were injured by the exploding door;

the rest gawked in dismay as the Rebels rushed them with guns drawn. Han took the lead, Leia right behind; Chewie covered the rear.

They herded all the personnel into one corner of the bunker. Three commandos guarded them there, three more covered the exits. The rest began placing the explosive charges.

Leia studied one of the screens on the control panel. "Hurry, Han, look! The fleet's being attacked!"

Solo looked over at the screen. "Blast it! With the shield still up, they're backed against the wall."

"That is correct," came a voice from the rear of the room. "Just as *you* are."

Han and Leia spun around to find dozens of Imperial guns trained on them; an entire legion had been hiding in the wall compartments of the bunker. Now, in a single moment, the Rebels were surrounded— nowhere to run, far too many stormtroopers to fight. Completely surrounded.

More Imperial troops charged through the door, roughly disarming the stunned commandos.

Han, Chewie, and Leia exchanged helpless, hope- less looks. They'd been the Rebellion's last chance.

They'd failed.

Some distance from the main area of battle, coasting safely in the center of the blanket of ships that consti- tuted the Imperial fleet, was the flagship Super Star Destroyer. On the bridge, Admiral Piett watched the war through the enormous observation window—cu- rious, as if viewing an elaborate demonstration, or an entertainment.

Two fleet captains stood behind him, respectfully silent; also learning the elegant designs of their Em- peror.

"Have the fleet hold here," Admiral Piett ordered.

The first captain hurried to carry out the order. The second stepped up to the window, beside the admiral. "We aren't going to attack?"

Piett smirked. "I have my orders from the Emperor

himself. He has something special planned for this
Rebel scum." He accented the specialness with a long
pause, for the inquisitive captain to savor. "We are only
to keep them from escaping."

The Emperor, Lord Vader, and Luke watched the
aerial battle rage from the safety of the throne room in
the Death Star.

It was a scene of pandemonium. Silent, crystalline
explosions surrounded by green, violet, or magenta au-
ras. Wildly vicious dogfights. Gracefully floating crags
of melted steel; icicle sprays that might have been
blood.

Luke watched in horror, as another Rebel ship toppled against the unseeable deflector shield, exploding
in a fiery concussion.

Vader watched Luke. His boy was powerful, stronger
than he'd imagined. And still pliable. Not lost yet—
either to the sickening, weakly side of the Force, that
had to beg for everything it received; or to the Emperor, who feared Luke with reason.

There was yet time to take Luke for his own—to
retake him. To join wih him in dark majesty. To rule
the galaxy together. It would cnly take patience and a
little wizardry, to show Luke the exquisite satisfactions
of the dark way and to pry him from the Emperor's
terrified clutch.

Vader knew Luke had seen it, too—the Emperor's
fear. He was a clever boy, young Luke, Vader smiled
grimly to himself. He was his father's son.

The Emperor interrupted Vader's contemplation
with a cackled remark to Luke. "As you can see, my
young apprentice, the deflector shield is still in place.
Your friends have failed! And now..." he raised his
spindly hand above his head to mark this moment:
"Witness the power of this fully armed and operational
battle station." He walked over to the comlink and
spoke in a gravelly whisper, as if to a lover. "Fire at
will, Commander."

In shock, and in foreknowledge, Luke looked out

across the surface of the Death Star, to the space battle beyond and to the bulk of the Rebel fleet beyond that.

Down in the bowels of the Death Star, Commander Jerjerrod gave an order. It was with mixed feelings that he issued the command, because it meant the final destruction of the Rebel insurrectionists—which meant an end to the state of war, which Jerjerrod cherished above all things. But second to ongoing war itself Jerjerrod loved total annihilation; so while tempered with regret, this order was not entirely without thrill.

At Jerjerrod's instruction, a controller pulled a switch, which ignited a blinking panel. Two hooded Imperial soldiers pushed a series of buttons. A thick beam of light slowly pulsed from a long, heavily blockaded shaft. On the outer surface of the completed half of the Death Star, a giant laser dish began to glow.

Luke watched in impotent horror, as the unbelievably huge laser beam radiated out from the muzzle of the Death Star. It touched—for only an instant—one of the Rebel Star Cruisers that was surging in the midst of the heaviest fighting. And in the next instant, the Star Cruiser was vaporized. Blown to dust. Returned to its most elemental particles, in a single burst of light.

In the numbing grip of despair, with the hollowest of voids devouring his heart, Luke's eyes, alone, glinted—for he saw, again, his lightsaber, lying unattended on the throne. And in this bleak and livid moment, the dark side was much with him.

 8

ADMIRAL Ackbar stood on the bridge in stunned disbelief, looking out the observation window at the place where, a moment before, the Rebel Star Cruiser *Liberty* had just been engaged in a furious long-range battle. Now, there was nothing. Only empty space, powdered with a fine dust that sparkled in the light of more distant explosions. Ackbar stared in silence.

Around him, confusion was rampant. Flustered controllers were still trying to contact the *Liberty*, while fleet captains ran from screen to port, shouting, directing, misdirecting.

An aide handed Ackbar the comlink. General Calrissian's voice was coming through.

"Home-one, this is Gold Leader. That blast came from the Death Star! Repeat, the Death Star is operational!"

"We saw it," Ackbar answered wearily. "All craft prepare to retreat."

"I'm not going to give up and run!" Lando shouted back. He'd come a long way to be in this game.

"We have no choice, General Calrissian. Our cruisers can't repel firepower of that magnitude!"

"You won't get a second chance at this, Admiral. Han will have that shield down—we've got to give him more time. Head for those Star Destroyers."

Ackbar looked around him. A huge charge of flak rumbled the ship, painting a brief, waxen light over the window. Calrissian was right: there would be no second chance. It was now, or it was the end.

He turned to his First Star captain. "Move the fleet forward."

"Yes, sir." The man paused. "Sir, we don't stand much of a chance against those Star Destroyers. They out-gun us, and they're more heavily armored."

"I know," Ackbar said softly.

The captain left. An aide approached.

"Forward ships have made contact with the Imperial fleet, sir."

"Concentrate your fire on their power generators. If we can knock out their shields, our fighters might stand a chance against them."

The ship was rocked by another explosion—a laserbolt hit to one of the aft gyrostabilizers.

"Intensify auxiliary shields!" someone yelled.

The pitch of the battle augmented another notch.

Beyond the window of the throne room, the Rebel fleet was being decimated in the soundless vacuum of space, while inside, the only sound was the Emperor's thready cackle. Luke continued his spiral into desperation as the Death Star laser beam incinerated ship after ship.

The Emperor hissed. "Your fleet is lost—and your friends on the Endor Moon will not survive..." He pushed a comlink button on the arm of his throne and spoke into it with relish. "Commander Jerjerrod, should the Rebels manage to blow up the shield generator, you will turn this battle station onto the Endor Moon and destroy it."

"Yes, Your Highness," came the voice over the receiver, "but we have several battalions stationed on—"

"You will destroy it!" the Emperor's whisper was more final than any scream.

"Yes, Your Highness."

Palpatine turned back to Luke—the former, shaking with glee; the latter, with outrage.

"There is no escape, my young pupil. The Alliance will die—as will your friends."

Luke's face was contorted, reflecting his spirit. Vader watched him carefully, as did the Emperor. The light-saber began to shake on its resting place. The young Jedi's hand was trembling, his lips pulled back in grimace, his teeth grinding.

The Emperor smiled. "Good. I can feel your anger. I am defenseless—take your weapon. Strike me down with all of your hatred, and your journey toward the dark side will be complete." He laughed, and laughed.

Luke was able to resist no longer. The lightsaber rattled violently on the throne a moment, then flew into his hand, impelled by the Force. He ignited it a moment later and swung it with his full weight downward toward the Emperor's skull.

In that instant, Vader's blade flashed into view, parrying Luke's attack an inch above the Emperor's head. Sparks flew like forging steel, bathing Palpatine's grinning face in a hellish glare.

Luke jumped back, and turned, lightsaber upraised, to face his father. Vader extended his own blade, poised to do battle.

The Emperor sighed with pleasure and sat in his throne, facing the combatants—the sole audience to this dire, aggrieved contest.

Han, Leia, Chewbacca, and the rest of the strike team were escorted out of the bunker by their captors. The sight that greeted them was substantially different from the way the grassy area had appeared when they'd entered. The clearing was now filled with Imperial troops.

Hundreds of them, in white or black armor—some

standing at ease, some viewing the scene from atop
their two-legged walkers, some leaning on their speeder
bikes. If the situation had appeared hopeless inside
the bunker, it looked even worse now.

Han and Leia turned to each other full of feeling.
All they'd struggled for, all they'd dreamed of—gone,
now. Even so, they'd had each other for a short while
at least. They'd come together from opposite ends of
a wasteland of emotional isolation: Han had never
known love, so enamored of himself was he; Leia had
never known love, so wrapped up in social upheaval
was she, so intent on embracing all of humanity. And
somewhere between his glassy infatuation for the one,
and her glowing fervor for the all, they'd found a shady
place where two could huddle, grow, even feel nourished.

But that, too, was cut short, now. The end seemed
near. So much was there to say, they couldn't find a
single word. Instead, they only joined hands, speaking
through their fingers in these final minutes of com-
panionship.

That's when Threepio and Artoo jauntily entered
the clearing, beeping and jabbering excitedly to each
other. They stopped cold in their tracks when they saw
what the clearing had become...and found all eyes
suddenly focused on them.

"Oh, dear," Threepio whimpered. In a second, he
and Artoo had turned around and run right back into
the woods from which they'd just come. Six stormtroopers charged in after them.

The Imperial soldiers were in time to see the two
droids duck behind a large tree, some twenty yards
into the forest. They rushed after the robots. As they
rounded the tree, they found Artoo and Threepio standing there quietly, waiting to be taken. The guards moved
to take them. They moved too slowly.

Fifteen Ewoks dropped out of the overhanging
branches, quickly overpowering the Imperial troops
with rocks and clubs. At that, Teebo—perched in an-

other tree—raised a ram's horn to his lips and sounded three long blasts from its bell. That was the signal for the Ewoks to attack.

Hundreds of them descended upon the clearing from all sides, throwing themselves against the might of the Imperial army with unrestrained zeal. The scene was unabridged chaos.

Stormtroopers fired their laser pistols at the furry creatures, killing or wounding many—only to be overrun by dozens more in their place. Biker scouts chased squealing Ewoks into the woods—and were knocked from their bikes by volleys of rocks launched from the trees.

In the first confused moments of the attack, Chewie dove into the foliage, while Han and Leia hit the dirt in the cover of the arches that flanked the bunker door. Explosions all around kept them pinned from leaving; the bunker door itself was closed again, and locked.

Han punched out the stolen code on the control panel keys—but this time, the door didn't open. It had been reprogrammed as soon as they'd been caught. "The terminal doesn't work now," he muttered.

Leia stretched for a laser pistol lying in the dirt, just out of reach, beside a felled stormtrooper. Shots were crisscrossing from every direction, though.

"We need Artoo," she shouted.

Han nodded, took out his comlink, pushed the sequence that signaled the little droid and reached for the weapon Leia couldn't get as the fighting stormed all around them.

Artoo and Threepio were huddled behind a log when Artoo got the message. He suddenly blurted out an excited whistle and shot off toward the battlefield.

"Artoo!" Threepio shouted. "Where are you going? Wait for me!" Nearly beside himself, the golden droid tore off after his best friend.

Biker scouts raced over and around the scurrying droids, blasting away at the Ewoks who grew fiercer every time their fur was scorched. The little bears were hanging on the legs of the Imperial walkers, hobbling the appendages with lengths of vine, or injuring the joint mechanisms by forcing pebbles and twigs into the hinges. They were knocking scouts off their bikes, by stringing vine between trees at throat level. They were throwing rocks, jumping out of trees, impaling with spears, entangling with nets. They were every- where.

Scores of them rallied behind Chewbacca, who had grown rather fond of them during the course of the previous night. He'd become their mascot; and they, his little country cousins. So it was with a special fe- rocity, now, that they came to each other's aid. Chewie was flinging stormtroopers left and right, in a selfless Wookiee frenzy, any time he saw them physically harming his small friends. The Ewoks, for their part, formed equally self-sacrificing cadres to do nothing but follow Chewbacca and throw themselves upon any sol- diers who started getting the upper hand with him.

It was a wild, strange battle.

Artoo and Threepio finally made it to the bunker door. Han and Leia provided cover fire with guns they'd finally managed to scrounge. Artoo moved quickly to the terminal, plugged in his computer arm, began scan- ning. Before he'd even computed the weather codes, though, a laser bolt explosion ripped the entranceway, disengaging Artoo's cable arm, spilling him to the dirt.

His head began to smolder, his fittings to leak. All of a sudden every compartment sprang open, every nozzle gushed or smoked, every wheel spun—and then stopped. Threepio rushed to his wounded companion, as Han examined the bunker terminal.

"Maybe I can hotwire this thing," Solo mumbled.

Meanwhile the Ewoks had erected a primitive cat- apult at the other side of the field. They fired a large boulder at one of the walkers—the machine vibrated seriously, but did not topple. It turned, and headed for the catapult, laser cannon firing. The Ewoks scattered. When the walker was ten feet away, the Ewoks chopped a mass of restraining vines, and two huge, balanced trunks crashed down on top of the Imperial war wagon, halting it for good.

The next phase of the assault began. Ewoks in kite-like animal-skin hang-gliders started dropping rocks on the stormtroopers, or dive-bombing with spears. Teebo, who led the attack, was hit in the wing with laser fire during the first volley and crashed into a gnarled root. A charging walker clumped forward to crush him, but Wicket swooped down just in time, yanking Teebo to safety. In swerving out of the walker's way, though, Wicket smashed into a racing speeder bike—they all went tumbling into the dense foliage.

And so it went.

The casualties mounted.

High above, it was no different. A thousand deadly dogfights and cannon bombardments were erupting all over the skies, while the Death Star laser beam methodically disintegrated the Rebel ships.

In the *Millennium Falcon*, Lando steered like a maniac through an obstacle course of the giant, floating Imperial Star Destroyers—trading laser bolts with them, dodging flak, outracing TIE fighters.

Desperately, he was shouting into his comlink, over the noise of continuous explosions, talking to Ackbar in the Alliance command ship. "I said *closer*! Move in as close as you can and engage the Star Destroyers at point blank range—that way the Death Star won't be able to fire at us without knocking out its own ships!"

"But no one's ever gone nose to nose at that range, between supervessels like their Destroyers and our Cruisers!" Ackbar fumed at the unthinkable—but their options were running out.

"Great!" yelled Lando, skimming over the surface of the Destroyer. "Then we're inventing a new kind of combat!"

"We know nothing about the tactics of such a confrontation!" Ackbar protested.

"We know as much as *they* do!" Lando hollered. "And they'll *think* we know more!" Bluffing was always dangerous in the last hand: but sometimes, when all your money was in the pot, it was the only way to win—and Lando never played to lose.

"At that close-range, we won't last long against Star Destroyers." Ackbar was already feeling giddy with resignation.

"We'll last longer than we will against that Death Star and we might just take a few of them with us!" Lando whooped. With a jolt, one of his forward guns was blown away. He put the *Falcon* into a controlled spin, and careened around the belly of the Imperial leviathan.

With little else to lose, Ackbar decided to try Calrissian's strategy. In the next minutes, dozens of Rebel Cruisers moved in astronomically close to the Imperial Star Destroyers—and the colossal antagonists began blasting away at each other, like tanks at twenty paces, while hundreds of tiny fighters raced across their surfaces, zipping between laser bolts as they chased around the massive hulls.

Slowly, Luke and Vader circled. Lightsaber high above his head, Luke readied his attack from classic first-position; the Dark Lord held a lateral stance, in classic answer. Without announcement, Luke brought his blade straight down—then, when Vader moved to parry, Luke feinted and cut low. Vader counterparried, let the impact direct his sword toward Luke's throat...but Luke met the riposte and stepped back. The first blows, traded without injury. Again, they circled.

Vader was impressed with Luke's speed. Pleased, even. It was a pity, almost, he couldn't let the boy kill the Emperor yet. Luke wasn't ready for that, emotionally. There was still a chance Luke would return to his friends if he destroyed the Emperor now. He needed more extensive tutelage, first—training by both Vader *and* Palpatine—before he'd be ready to assume his place at Vader's right hand, ruling the galaxy.

So Vader had to shepherd the boy through periods

like this, stop him from doing damage in the wrong places—or in the right places prematurely.

Before Vader could gather his thoughts much further, though, Luke attacked again—much more aggressively. He advanced in a flurry of lunges, each met with a loud crack of Vader's phosphorescent saber. The Dark Lord retreated a step at every slash, swiveling once to bring his cutting beam up viciously—but Luke batted it away, pushing Vader back yet again. The Lord of the Sith momentarily lost his footing on the stairs and tumbled to his knees.

Luke stood above him, at the top of the staircase, heady with his own power. It was in his hands, now, he knew it was: he could take Vader. Take his blade, take his life. Take his place at the Emperor's side. Yes, even that. Luke didn't bury the thought, this time; he gloried in it. He engorged himself with its juices, felt its power tingle his cheeks. It made him feverish, this thought, with lust so overpowering as to totally obliterate all other considerations.

He had the power; the choice was his.

And then another thought emerged, slowly compulsive as an ardent lover: he could destroy the Emperor, too. Destroy them both, and rule the galaxy. Avenge and conquer.

It was a profound moment for Luke. Dizzying. Yet he did not swoon. Nor did he recoil.

He took one step forward.

For the first time, the thought entered Vader's consciousness that his son might best him. He was astounded by the strength Luke had acquired since their last duel, in the Cloud City—not to mention the boy's timing, which was honed to a thought's-breadth. This was an unexpected circumstance. Unexpected and unwelcome. Vader felt humiliation crawling in on the tail of his first reaction, which was surprise, and his second, which was fear. And then the edge of the humiliation curled up, to reveal bald anger. And now he wanted revenge.

These things were mirrored, each facet, by the young

Jedi who now towered above him. The Emperor, watching joyously, saw this, and goaded Luke on to revel in his Darkness. "Use your aggressive feelings, boy! Yes! Let the hate flow through you! Become one with it, let it nourish you!"

Luke faltered a moment—then realized what was happening. He was suddenly confused again. What did he want? What should he do? His brief exultation, his microsecond of dark clarity—gone, now, in a wash of indecision, veiled enigma. Cold awakening from a passionate flirtation.

He took a step back, lowered his sword, relaxed, and tried to drive the hatred from his being.

In that instant, Vader attacked. He lunged half up the stairs, forcing Luke to reverse defensively. He bound the boy's blade with his own, but Luke disengaged and leaped to the safety of an overhead gantry. Vader jumped over the railing to the floor beneath the platform on which Luke stood.

"I will not fight you, Father," Luke stated.

"You are unwise to lower your defenses," Vader warned. His anger was layered, now—he did not want to win if the boy was not battling to the fullest. But if winning meant he had to kill a boy who wouldn't fight...then he could do that, too. Only he wanted Luke to be aware of those consequences. He wanted Luke to know this was no longer just a game. This was Darkness.

Luke heard something else, though. "Your thoughts betray you, Father. I feel the good in you...the conflict. You could not bring yourself to kill me before— and you won't destroy me now." Twice before, in fact— to Luke's recollection—Vader could have killed him, but didn't. In the dogfight over the first Death Star, and later in the lightsaber duel on Bespin. He thought of Leia, briefly now, too—of how Vader had had *her* in his clutches once, had even tortured her...but didn't kill her. He winced to think of her agony, but quickly pushed that from his mind. The point was clear to him, now, though so often so murky: there was still good in his father.

This accusation *really* made Vader angry. He could tolerate much from the insolent child, but this was insufferable. He must teach this boy a lesson he would never forget, or die learning. "Once again, you underestimate the power of the dark side..."

Vader threw his scintillating blade—it sliced through the supports holding up the gantry on which Luke was perched, then swept around and flew back into Vader's hand. Luke tumbled to the ground, then rolled down another level, under the tilting platform. In the shadow of the darkened overhang, he was out of sight. Vader paced the area like a cat, seeking the boy; but he wouldn't enter the shadows of the overhang.

"You cannot hide forever, Luke."

"You'll have to come in and get me," replied the disembodied voice.

"I will not give you the advantage that easily." Vader felt his intentions increasingly ambiguous in this conflict; the purity of his evil was being compromised. The boy was clever indeed—Vader knew he must move with extreme caution now.

"I wish no advantage, father. I will not fight you. Here...take my weapon." Luke knew full well this might be his end, but so be it. He would not use Darkness to fight Darkness. Perhaps it would be left to Leia, after all, to carry on the struggle, without him. Perhaps she would know a way he didn't know; perhaps she could find a path. For now, though, he could see only two paths, and one was into Darkness; and one was not.

Luke put his lightsaber on the ground, and rolled it along the floor toward Vader. It stopped halfway between them, in the middle of the low overhead area. The Dark Lord reached out his hand—Luke's lightsaber jumped into it. He hooked it to his belt and, with grave uncertainty, entered the shadowy overhang.

He was picking up additional feelings from Luke,

now, new crosscurrents of doubt. Remorse, regret, abandonment. Shades of pain. But somehow not directly related to Vader. To others, to...Endor. Ah, that was it—the Sanctuary Moon where his friends would soon die. Luke would learn soon enough: friendship was different on the dark side. A different thing altogether.

"Give yourself to the dark side, Luke," he entreated. "It is the only way you can save your friends. Yes, your thoughts betray you, son. Your feelings for them are strong, especially for—"

Vader stopped. He sensed something.

Luke withdrew further into shadow. He tried to hide, but there was no way to hide what was in his mind— Leia was in pain. Her agony cried to him now, and his spirit cried with her. He tried to shut it out, to shut it up, but the cry was loud, and he couldn't stifle it, couldn't leave it alone, had to cradle it openly, to give it solace.

Vader's consciousness invaded that private place.

"No!" screamed Luke.

Vader was incredulous. "Sister? Sister!" he bellowed. "Your feelings have now betrayed her, too... Twins!" he roared triumphantly. "Obi-Wan was wise to hide her, but now his failure is complete." His smile was clear to Luke, through the mask, through the shadows, through all the realms of Darkness. "If you will not turn to the Dark Side, perhaps she will."

This, then, was Luke's breaking point. For Leia was everyone's last unflagging hope. If Vader turned his twisted, misguided cravings on her...

"Never!" he screamed. His lightsaber flew off Vader's belt into his own hand, igniting as it came to him.

He rushed to his father with a frenzy he'd never known. Nor had Vader. The gladiators battled fiercely, sparks flying from the clash of their radiant weapons, but it was soon evident that the advantage was all Luke's. And he was pressing it. They locked swords, body to body. When Luke pushed Vader back to break the clinch, the Dark Lord hit his head on an overhanging beam in the cramped space. He stumbled backward even farther, out of the low-hanging area. Luke pursued him relentlessly.

Blow upon blow, Luke forced Vader to retreat—back, onto the bridge that crossed the vast, seemingly bottomless shaft to the power core. Each stroke of Luke's saber pummeled Vader, like accusations, like screams, like shards of hate.

The Dark Lord was driven to his knees. He raised his blade to block yet another onslaught—and Luke slashed Vader's right hand off at the wrist.

The hand, along with bits of metal, wires, and electronic devices, clattered uselessly away while Vader's lightsaber tumbled over the edge of the span, into the endless shaft below, without a trace.

Luke stared at his father's twitching, severed, mechanical hand—and then at his own black-gloved artificial part—and realized suddenly just how much he'd become like his father. Like the man he hated.

Trembling, he stood above Vader, the point of his glowing blade at the Dark Lord's throat. He wanted to destroy this thing of Darkness, this thing that was once his father, this thing that was ... him.

Suddenly the Emperor was there, looking on, chuckling with uncontrollable, pleased agitation. "Good! Kill him! Your hate has made you powerful! Now, fulfill your destiny and take your father's place at my side!"

Luke stared at his father beneath him, then at the Emperor, then back at Vader. This was Darkness—and it was the *Darkness* he hated. Not his father, not even the Emperor. But the Darkness *in* them. In them, and in himself.

And the only way to destroy the Darkness was to renounce it. For good and all. He stood suddenly erect, and made the decision for which he'd spent his life in preparation.

He hurled his lightsaber away. "Never! Never will I turn to the dark side! You have failed, Palpatine. I am a Jedi, as my father was before me."

The Emperor's glee turned to a sullen rage. "So be

it, Jedi. If you will not be turned, you will be destroyed."

Palpatine raised his spidery arms toward Luke: blinding white bolts of energy coruscated from his fingers, shot across the room like sorcerous lightning, and tore through the boy's insides, looking for ground. The young Jedi was at once confounded and in agony— he'd never heard of such a power, such a corruption of the Force, let alone experienced it.

But if it was Force-generated, it could be Force-repelled. Luke raised his arms to deflect the bolts. Initially, he was successful—the lightning rebounded from his touch, harmlessly into the walls. Soon, though, the shocks came with such speed and power, they coursed over and into him, and he could only shrink before them, convulsed with pain, his knees buckling, his powers at ebb.

Vader crawled, like a wounded animal, to his Emperor's side.

On Endor, the battle of the bunker continued. Stormtroopers kept irradiating Ewoks with sophisticated weaponry, while the fuzzy little warriors bashed away at the Imperial troops with clubs, tumbled walkers with logpiles and vine trip-wires, lassoed speeder bikes with vine-ropes and net-traps.

They felled trees on their foes. They dug pits which they covered with branches, and then lured the walkers to chase them until the clumsy armored vehicles toppled into the dug-outs. They started rockslides. They dammed a small, nearby stream, and then opened the floodgates, deluging a host of troops and two more walkers. They ganged up, and then ran away. They jumped on top of walkers from high branches, and poured pouches of burning lizard-oil in the gun-slits. They used knives, and spears, and slings, and made scary war-shrieks to confound and dismay the enemy. They were fearless opponents.

Their example made even Chewie bolder than was his wont. He started having so much fun swinging on vines and bashing heads, he nearly forgot about his laser pistol.

He swung onto the roof of a Walker at one point, with Teebo and Wicket clinging to his back. They landed with a thud atop the lurching contraption, then made such a banging racket trying to hang on, one of the stormtroopers inside opened the top hatch to see what was happening. Before he could fire his gun, Chewie plucked him out and dashed him to the ground—Wicket and Teebo immediately dove into the hatch and subdued the other trooper.

Ewoks drive an Imperial Walker much the way they drive speeder bikes—terribly, but with exhilaration. Chewie was almost thrown off the top several times, but even barking angrily down into the cockpit didn't seem to have much effect—the Ewoks just giggled, squealed, and careened into another speeder bike.

Chewie climbed down inside. It took him half a minute to master the controls—Imperial technology was pretty standardized. And then, methodically, one by one, he began approaching the other, unsuspecting, Imperial Walkers, and blasting them to dust. Most had no idea what was happening.

As the giant war-machines began going up in flames, the Ewoks were reinspired. They rallied behind Chewie's Walker. The Wookiee was turning the tide of battle.

Han, meanwhile, was still working furiously at the control panel. Wires sparked each time he refastened another connection, but the door kept not opening. Leia crouched at his back, firing her laser pistol, giving him cover.

He motioned her at last. "Give me a hand, I think I've got it figured out. Hold this."

He handed her one of the wires. She holstered her weapon, took the wire he gave her, and held it in position as he brought two others over from opposite ends of the panel.

"Here goes nothing," he said.

The three wires sparked; the connection was made. There was a sudden loud WHUMP, as a second blast door crashed down in front of the first, doubling the impregnable barrier.

"Great. Now we have two doors to get through," Leia muttered.

At that moment, she was hit in the arm by a laser bolt, and knocked to the ground.

Han rushed over to her. "Leia, no!" he cried, trying to stop the bleeding.

"Princess Leia, are you all right?" Threepio fretted.

"It's not bad," she shook her head. "It's—"

"Hold it!" shouted a voice. "One move and you're both dead!"

They froze, looked up. Two stormtroopers stood before them, weapons leveled, unwavering.

"Stand up," one ordered. "Hands raised."

Han and Leia looked at each other, fixed their gazes deep in each other's eyes, swam there in the wells of their souls for a suspended, eternal moment, during which all was felt, understood, touched, shared.

Solo's gaze was drawn down to Leia's holster—she'd surreptitiously eased out her gun, and was holding it now at the ready. The action was hidden from the troopers, because Han was standing in front of Leia, half-blocking their view.

He looked again into her eyes, comprehending. With a last, heartfelt smile, he whispered, "I love you."

"I know," she answered simply.

Then the moment was over; and at an unspoken, instantaneous signal, Han whirled out of the line of fire as Leia blasted at the stormtroopers.

The air was filled with laser fire—a glinting orange-pink haze, like an electron storm, buffeted the area, sheared by intense flares.

As the smoke cleared, a giant Imperial Walker approached, stood before him, and stopped. Han looked up to see its laser cannons aimed directly in his face. He raised his arms, and took a tentative step forward. He wasn't really sure what he was going to do. "Stay back," he said quietly to Leia, measuring the distance to the machine, in his mind.

That was when the hatch on top of the Walker popped open and Chewbacca stuck his head out with an ingratiating smile.

"Ahr Rahr!" barked the Wookiee.

Solo could have kissed him. "Chewie! Get down here! She's wounded!" He started forward to greet his partner, then stopped in mid-stride. "No, wait. I've got an idea."

 9

THE two space armadas, like their sea-bound counterparts of another time and galaxy, sat floating, ship to ship, trading broadsides with each other in point-blank confrontation.

Heroic, sometimes suicidal, maneuvers marked the day. A Rebel cruiser, its back alive with fires and explosions, limped into direct contact with an Imperial Star Destroyer before exploding completely—taking the Star Destroyer with it. Cargo ships loaded with charge were set on collision courses with fortress-vessels, their crews abandoning ships to fates that were uncertain, at best.

Lando, Wedge, Blue Leader, and Green Wing went in to take out one of the larger Destroyers—the Empire's main communications ship. It had already been disabled by direct cannonade from the Rebel cruiser it had subsequently destroyed; but its damages were reparable—so the Rebels had to strike while it was still licking its wounds.

Lando's squadron went in low—rock-throwing low—this prevented the Destroyer from using its bigger guns. It also made the fighters invisible until they were directly visualized.

"Increase power on the front deflector shields," Lando radioed his group. "We're going in."

"I'm right with you," answered Wedge. "Close up formations, team."

They went into a high-speed power-dive, perpendicular to the long axis of the Imperial vessel—vertical drops were hard to track. Fifty feet from the surface, they pulled out at ninety degrees, and raced along the gunmetal hull, taking laserfire from every port.

"Starting attack run on the main power tree," Lando advised.

"I copy," answered Green Wing. "Moving into position."

"Stay clear of their front batteries," warned Blue Leader.

"It's a heavy fire zone down there."

"I'm in range."

"She's hurt bad on the left of the tower," Wedge noted. "Concentrate on that side."

"Right with you."

Green Wing was hit. "I'm losing power!"

"Get clear, you're going to blow!"

Green Wing took it down like riding a rocket, into the Destroyer's front batteries. Tremendous explosions rumbled the port bow.

"Thanks," Blue Leader said quietly to the conflagration.

"That opens it up for us!" yelled Wedge. "Cut over. The power reactors are just inside that cargo bay."

"Follow me!" Lando called, pulling the *Falcon* into a sharp bank that caught the horrified reactor personnel by surprise. Wedge and Blue followed suit. They all did their worst.

"Direct hit!" Lando shouted.

"There she goes!"

"Pull up, pull up!"

They pulled up hard and fast, as the Destroyer was enveloped in a series of ever-increasing explosions, until it looked finally just like one more small star. Blue Leader was caught by the shock wave, and thrown horribly against the side of a smaller Imperial ship, which also exploded. Lando and Wedge escaped.

On the Rebel command ship bridge, smoke and shouts filled the air.

Ackbar reached Calrissian on the comlink. "The jamming has stopped. We have a reading on the shield."

"Is it still up?" Lando responded with desperate anticipation in his voice.

"I'm afraid so. It looks like General Solo's unit didn't make it."

"Until they've destroyed our last ship, there's still hope," replied Lando. Han wouldn't fail. He couldn't— they still had to pick off that annoying Death Star.

On the Death Star, Luke was nearly unconscious beneath the continuing assault of the Emperor's light-ning. Tormented beyond reason, betaken of a weak-ness that drained his very essence, he hoped for nothing more than to submit to the nothingness toward which he was drifting.

The Emperor smiled down at the enfeebled young Jedi, as Vader struggled to his feet beside his master.

"Young fool!" Palpatine rasped at Luke. "Only now at the end, do you understand. Your puerile skills are no match for the power of the dark side. You have paid a price for your lack of vision. Now, young Skywalker, you will pay the price in full. You will die!"

He laughed maniacally; and although it would not have seemed possible to Luke, the outpouring of bolts from the Emperor's fingers actually increased in in-tensity. The sound screamed through the room, the murderous brightness of the flashes was overwhelm-ing.

Luke's body slowed, wilted, finally crumpled under the hideous barrage. He stopped moving altogether.

At last, he appeared totally lifeless. The Emperor hissed maliciously.

At that instant, Vader sprang up and grabbed the Emperor from behind, pinning Palpatine's upper arms to his torso. Weaker than he'd ever been, Vader had lain still these last few minutes, focusing his every fiber of being on this one, concentrated act—the only action possible; his last, if he failed. Ignoring pain, ignoring his shame and his weaknesses, ignoring the bone-crushing noise in his head, he focused solely and sight-lessly on his will—his will to defeat the evil embodied in the Emperor.

Palpatine struggled in the grip of Vader's unfeeling embrace, his hands still shooting bolts of malign energy out in all directions. In his wild flailing, the light-ning ripped across the room, tearing into Vader. The Dark Lord fell again, electric currents crackling down his helmet, over his cape, into his heart.

Vader stumbled with his load to the middle of the bridge over the black chasm leading to the power core. He held the wailing despot high over his head, and with a final spasm of strength, hurled him into the abyss.

Palpatine's body, still spewing bolts of light, spun out of control, into the void, bouncing back and forth off the sides of the shaft as it fell. It disappeared at last; but then, a few seconds later, a distant explosion could be heard, far down at the core. A rush of air billowed out the shaft, into the throne room.

The wind whipped at Lord Vader's cape, as he stag-gered and collapsed toward the hole, trying to follow his master to the end. Luke crawled to his father's side, though, and pulled the Dark Lord away from the edge of the chasm, to safety.

Both of them lay on the floor, entwined in each other, too weak to move, too moved to speak.

Inside the bunker on Endor, Imperial controllers watched the main view-screen of the Ewok battle just outside. Though the image was clogged with static, the fighting seemed to be winding down. About time, since they'd initially been told that the locals on this moon were harmless nonbelligerents.

The interference seemed to worsen—probably another antenna damaged in the fighting—when suddenly a walker pilot appeared on the screen, waving excitedly.

"It's over, Commander! The Rebels have been routed, and are fleeing with the bear-creatures into the woods. We need reinforcements to continue the pursuit."

The bunker personnel all cheered. The shield was safe.

"Open the main door!" ordered the commander. "Send three squads to help."

The bunker door opened, the Imperial troops came rushing out only to find themselves surrounded by Rebels and Ewoks, looking bloody and mean. The Imperial troops surrendered without a fight.

Han, Chewie, and five others ran into the bunker with the explosive charges. They placed the timed devices at eleven strategic points in and around the power generator, then ran out again as fast as they could.

Leia, still in great pain from her wounds, lay in the sheltered comfort of some distant bushes. She was shouting orders to the Ewoks, to gather their prisoners on the far side of the clearing, away from the bunker when Han and Chewie tore out, racing for cover. In the next moment, the bunker went.

It was a spectacular display, explosion after explosion sending a wall of fire hundreds of feet into the air, creating a shock wave that knocked every living creature off its feet, and charred all the greenery that faced the clearing.

The bunker was destroyed.

A captain ran up to Admiral Ackbar, his voice tremulous. "Sir, the shield around the Death Star has lost its power."

Ackbar looked at the view-screen; the electronically

generated web was gone. The moon, and the Death Star, now floated in black, empty, unprotected space.

"They did it," Ackbar whispered.

He rushed over to the comlink and shouted into the multifrequency war channel. "All fighters commence attack on the Death Star's main reactor. The deflector shield is down. Repeat. The deflector shield is down!"

Lando's voice was the next one heard. "I see it. We're on our way. Red group! Gold group! Blue Squad! All fighters follow me!" That's my man, Han. Now it's my turn.

The *Falcon* plunged to the surface of the Death Star, followed by hordes of Rebel fighters, followed by a still-massing but disorganized array of Imperial TIE fighters—while three Rebel Star Cruisers headed for the huge Imperial Super Star Destroyer, Vader's flagship, which seemed to be having difficulties with its guidance system.

Lando and the first wave of X-wings headed for the unfinished portion of the Death Star, skimming low over the curving surface of the completed side.

"Stay low until we get to the unfinished side," Wedge told his squad. Nobody needed to be told.

"Squadron of enemy fighters coming—"

"Blue Wing," called Lando, "take your group and draw the TIE fighters away—"

"I'll do what I can."

"I'm picking up interference...the Death Star's jamming us, I think—"

"More fighters coming at ten o'clock—"

"There's the superstructure," Lando called. "Watch for the main reactor shaft."

He turned hard into the unfinished side, and began weaving dramatically among protruding girders, half-built towers, mazelike channels, temporary scaffolding, sporadic floodlights. The antiaircraft defenses weren't nearly as well developed here yet—they'd been depending completely on the deflector shield for protection. Consequently the major sources of worry for the Rebels were the physical jeopardies of the structure itself, and the Imperial TIE fighters on their tails.

"I see it—the power-channel system," Wedge radioed. "I'm going in."

"I see it, too," agreed Lando. "Here goes nothing."

"This isn't going to be easy—"

Over a tower and under a bridge—and suddenly they were flying at top speed inside a deep shaft that was barely wide enough for three fighters, wing to wing. Moreover, it was pierced, along its entire twisting length, by myriad feeding shafts and tunnels, alternate forks, and dead-end caverns; and spiked, in addition, with an alarming number of obstacles *within* the shaft itself: heavy machinery, structural elements, power cables, floating stairways, barrier half-walls, piled debris.

A score of Rebel fighters made the first turn-off into the power shaft, followed by twice that number of TIEs. Two X-wings lost it right away, careening into a derrick to avoid the first volley of laser fire.

The chase was on.

"Where are we going, Gold Leader?" Wedge called out gaily. A laserbolt hit the shaft above him, showering his window with sparks.

"Lock onto the strongest power source," Lando suggested. "It should be the generator."

"Red Wing, stay alert—we could run out of space real fast."

They quickly strung out into single and double file, as it started becoming apparent that the shaft was not only pocked with side-vents and protruding obstacles, but also narrowing across its width at every turn.

TIE fighters hit another Rebel, who exploded in flames. Then another TIE fighter hit a piece of machinery, with a similar result.

"I've got a reading on a major shaft obstruction ahead," Lando announced.

"Just picked it up. Will you make it?"

"Going to be a tight squeeze."

It was a tight squeeze. It was a heat-wall occluding three fourths of the tunnel, with a dip in the shaft at the same level to make up a little room. Lando had to spin the *Falcon* through 360 degrees while rising, falling, and accelerating. Luckily, the X-wings and Y-wings weren't quite as bulky. Still, two more of them didn't make it on the downside. The smaller TIEs drew closer.

Suddenly coarse white static blanketed all the view-screens.

"My scope's gone!" yelled Wedge.

"Cut speed," cautioned Lando. "Some kind of power discharge causing interference."

"Switch to visual scanning."

"That's useless at these velocities—we'll have to fly nearly blind."

Two blind X-wings hit the wall as the shaft narrowed again. A third was blown apart by the gaining Imperial fighters.

"Green Leader!" called Lando.

"Copy, Gold Leader."

"Split off and head back to the suface—Home-one just called for a fighter, and you might draw some fire off us."

Green Leader and his cohort peeled off, out of the power shaft, back up to the cruiser battle. One TIE fighter followed, firing continuously.

Ackbar's voice came in over the comlink. "The Death Star is turning away from the fleet—looks like it's repositioning to destroy the Endor Moon."

"How long before it's in position?" Lando asked.

"Point oh three."

"That's not enough time! We're running out of time."

Wedge broke in the transmission. "Well, we're running out of shaft, too."

At that instant the *Falcon* scraped through an even smaller opening, this time injuring her auxiliary thrusters.

"That was too close," muttered Calrissian.

"Gdzhng dzn," nodded the copilot.

Ackbar stared wild-eyed out the observation window. He was looking down onto the deck of the Super

Star Destroyer; only miles away. Fires burst over the entire stern, and the Imperial warship was listing badly to starboard.

"We've knocked out their forward shields," Ackbar said into the comlink. "Fire at the bridge."

Green Leader's group swooped in low, from bottomside, up from the Death Star.

"Glad to help out, Home-one," called Green Leader.

"Firing proton torpedoes," Green Wing advised.

The bridge was hit, with kaleidoscopic results. A rapid chain reaction got set off, from power station to power station along the middle third of the huge Destroyer, producing a dazzling rainbow of explosions that buckled the ship at right angles, and started it spinning like a pinwheel toward the Death Star.

The first bridge explosion took Green Leader with it; the subsequent uncontrolled joyride snagged ten more fighters, two cruisers, and an ordnance vessel. By the time the whole exothermic conglomerate finally crashed into the side of the Death Star, the impact was momentous enough to actually jolt the battle station, setting off internal explosions and thunderings all through its network of reactors, munitions, and halls.

For the first time, the Death Star rocked. The collision with the exploding Destroyer was only the beginning, leading to various systems breakdowns, which led to reactor meltdowns, which led to personnel panic, abandonment of posts, further malfunctions, and general chaos.

Smoke was everywhere, substantial rumblings came from all directions at once, people were running and shouting. Electrical fires, steam explosions, cabin depressurizations, disruption of chain-of-command. Added to this, the continued bombardments by Rebel cruisers—smelling fear in the enemy—merely heightened the sense of hysteria that was already pervasive.

For the Emperor was dead. The central, powerful evil that had been the cohesive force to the Empire was gone; and when the dark side was this diffused, this nondirected—this was simply where it led.

Confusion.

Desperation.

Damp fear.

In the midst of this uproar, Luke had made it, somehow, to the main docking bay—where he was trying to carry the hulking deadweight of his father's weakening body toward an Imperial shuttle. Halfway there, his strength finally gave out, though; and he collapsed under the strain.

Slowly he rose again. Like an automaton, he hoisted his father's body over his shoulder and stumbled toward one of the last remaining shuttles.

Luke rested his father on the ground, trying to collect strength one last time, as explosions grew louder all around them. Sparks hissed in the rafters; one of the walls buckled, and smoke poured through a gaping fissure. The floor shook.

Vader motioned Luke closer to him. "Luke, help me take this mask off."

Luke shook his head. "You'll die."

The Dark Lord's voice was weary. "Nothing can stop that now. Just once let me face you without it. Let me look on you with my own eyes."

Luke was afraid. Afraid to see his father as he really was. Afraid to see what person could have become so dark—the same person who'd fathered Luke, and Leia. Afraid to know the Anakin Skywalker who lived inside Darth Vader.

Vader, too, was afraid—to let his son see him, to remove this armored mask that had been between them so long. The black, armored mask that had been his only means of existing for over twenty years. It had been his voice, and his breath, and his invisibility— his shield against all human contact. But now he would remove it; for he would see his son before he died.

Together they lifted the heavy helmet from Vader's head—inside the mask portion, a complicated breath-

ing apparatus had to be disentangled, a speaking mod-
ulator and view-screen detached from the power unit
in back. But when the mask was finally off and set
aside, Luke gazed on his father's face.

It was the sad, benign face of an old man. Bald,
beardless, with a mighty scar running from the top of
his head to the back of the scalp, he had unfocused,
deepset, dark eyes, and his skin was pasty white, for
it had not seen the sun in two decades. The old man
smiled weakly; tears glazed his eyes, now. For a moment, he looked not too unlike Ben.

It was a face full of meanings, that Luke would forever recall. Regret, he saw most plainly. And shame.
Memories could be seen flashing across it...memories
of rich times. And horrors. And love, too.

It was a face that hadn't touched the world in a
lifetime. In Luke's lifetime. He saw the wizened nostrils twitch, as they tested a first, tentative smell. He
saw the head tilt imperceptibly to listen—for the first
time without electronic auditory amplification. Luke
felt a pang of remorse that the only sounds now to be
heard were those of explosions, the only smells, the
pungent sting of electrical fires. Still, it was a touch.
Palpable, unfiltered.

He saw the old eyes focus on him. Tears burned
Luke's cheeks, fell on his father's lips. His father smiled
at the taste.

It was a face that had not seen itself in twenty years.

Vader saw his son crying, and knew it must have
been at the horror of the face the boy beheld.

It intensified, momentarily, Vader's own sense of
anguish—to his crimes, now, he added guilt at the
imagined repugnance of his appearance. But then this
brought him to mind of the way he used to look—
striking, and grand, with a wry tilt to his brow that
hinted of invincibility and took in all of life with a wink.
Yes, that was how he'd looked once.

And this memory brought a wave of other memories
with it. Memories of brotherhood, and home. His dear
wife. The freedom of deep space. Obi-Wan.

Obi-Wan, his friend...and how that friendship had turned. Turned, he knew not how—but got injected, nonetheless, with some uncaring virulence that festered, until...hold. These were memories he wanted none of, not now. Memories of molten lava, crawling up his back...no.

This boy had pulled him from that pit—here, now, with this act. This boy was good.

The boy was good, and the boy had come from *him*—so there must have been good in *him*, too. He smiled up again at his son, and for the first time, loved him. And for the first time in many long years, loved himself again, as well.

Suddenly he smelled something—flared his nostrils, sniffed once more. Wildflowers, that was what it was. Just blooming; it must be spring.

And there was thunder—he cocked his head, strained his ears. Yes, spring thunder, for a spring rain. To make the flowers bloom.

Yes, there...he felt a raindrop on his lips. He licked the delicate droplet...but wait, it wasn't sweetwater, it was salty, it was...a teardrop.

He focused on Luke once again, and saw his son was crying. Yes that was it, he was tasting his boy's grief—because he looked so horrible; because he *was* so horrible.

But he wanted to make it all right for Luke, he wanted Luke to know he wasn't really ugly like this, not deep inside, not all together. With a little self-deprecatory smile, he shook his head at Luke, explaining away the unsightly beast his son saw. "Luminous beings are we, Luke—not this crude matter."

Luke shook his head, too—to tell his father it was all right, to dismiss the old man's shame, to tell him nothing mattered now. And everything—but he couldn't talk.

Vader spoke again, even weaker—almost inaudible. "Go, my son. Leave me."

At that, Luke found his voice. "No. You're coming with me. I'll not leave you here. I've got to save you."

"You already have, Luke," he whispered. He wished, briefly, he'd met Yoda, to thank the old Jedi for the training he'd given Luke...but perhaps he'd be with Yoda soon, now, in the ethereal oneness of the Force. And with Obi-Wan.

"Father, I won't leave you," Luke protested. Explosions jarred the docking bay in earnest, crumbling one entire wall, splitting the ceiling. A jet of blue flame shot from a gas nozzle nearby. Just beneath it the floor began to melt.

Vader pulled Luke very close, spoke into his ear. "Luke, you were right...and you were right about me...Tell your sister...you were right."

With that, he closed his eyes, and Darth Vader—Anakin Skywalker—died.

A tremendous explosion filled the back of the bay with fire, knocking Luke flat to the ground. Slowly, he rose again; and like an automaton, stumbled toward one of the last remaining shuttles.

The *Millennium Falcon* continued its swerving race through the labyrinth of power channels, inching ever-closer to the hub of the giant sphere—the main reactor. The Rebel cruisers were unloading a continuous bombardment on the exposed, unfinished superstructure of the Death Star, now, each hit causing a resonating shudder in the immense battle station, and a new series of catastrophic events within.

Commander Jerjerrod sat, brooding, in the control room of the Death Star, watching all about him crumble. Half of his crew were dead, wounded, or run off—where they hoped to find sanctuary was unclear, if not insane. The rest wandered ineffectually, or railed at the enemy ships, or fired all their guns at all sectors, or shouted orders, or focused desperately on a single task, as if that would save them. Or, like Jerjerrod, simply brooded.

He couldn't fathom what he'd done wrong. He'd been patient, he'd been loyal, he'd been clever, he'd been hard. He was the commander of the greatest bat-

tle station ever built. Or, at least, almost built. He hated
this Rebel Alliance, now, with a child's hate, untem-
pered. He'd loved it once—it had been the small boy
he could bully, the enraged baby animal he could torture. But the boy had grown up now; it knew how to
fight back effectively. It had broken its bonds.

Jerjerrod hated it now.

Yet there seemed to be little he could do at this
point. Except, of course, destroy Endor—he could do
that. It was a small act, a token really—to incinerate
something green and living, gratuitously, meanly, toward no end but that of wanton destruction. A small
act, but deliciously satisfying.

An aide ran up to him. "The Rebel fleet is closing,
sir."

"Concentrate all fire in that sector," he answered
distractedly. A console on the far wall burst into flame.

"The fighters in the superstructure are eluding our
defense system, Commander. Shouldn't we—"

"Flood sectors 304 and 138. That should slow them
up." He arched his eyebrows at the aide.

This made little sense to the aide, who had cause
to wonder at the commander's grasp of the situation.
"But sir..."

"What is the rotation factor to firing range on the
Endor Moon?"

The aide checked the compuscreen. "Point oh two
to moon target, sir. Commander, the fleet—"

"Accelerate rotation until moon is in range, and then
fire on my mark."

"Yes, sir." The aide pulled a bank of switches. "Rotation accelerating, sir. Point oh one to moon target,
sir. Sixty seconds to firing range. Sir, good-bye, sir."
The aide saluted, put the firing switch in Jerjerrod's
hand as another explosion shook the control room, and
ran out the door.

Jerjerrod smiled calmly at the view-screen. Endor
was starting to come out of the Death Star's eclipse.
He fondled the detonation switch in his hand. Point

oh oh five to moon target. Screams erupted in the next room.

Thirty seconds to firing.

Lando was homing in on the reactor core shaft. Else only Wedge was left, flying just ahead of him, and Gold Wing, just behind. Several TIE fighters still trailed.

These central twistings were barely two planes wide, and turned sharply every five or ten seconds at the speeds Lando was reaching. Another Imperial jet exploded against a wall; another shot down Gold Wing.

And then there were two.

Lando's tail-gunners kept the remaining TIE fighters jumping in the narrow space, until at last the main reactor shaft came into view. They'd never seen a reactor that awesome.

"It's too big, Gold Leader," yelled Wedge. "My proton torpedoes won't even dent that."

"Go for the power regulator on the north tower," Lando directed. "I'll take the main reactor. We're carrying concussion missiles—they should penetrate. Once I let them go, we won't have much time to get out of here, though."

"I'm already on my way out," Wedge exclaimed.

He fired his torpedoes with a Corellian war-cry, hitting both sides of the north tower, and peeled off, accelerating.

The *Falcon* waited three dangerous seconds longer, then loosed its concussion missiles with a powerful roar. For another second the flash was too bright to see what had happened. And then the whole reactor began to go.

"Direct hit!" shouted Lando. "Now comes the hard part."

The shaft was already caving in on top of him, creating a tunnel effect. The *Falcon* maneuvered through the twisting outlet, through walls of flame, and through moving shafts, always just ahead of the continuing chain of explosions.

Wedge tore out of the superstructure at barely sublight speed, whipped around the near side of Endor, and coasted into deep space, slowing slowly in a gentle arc, to return to the safety of the moon.

A moment later, in a destabilized Imperial shuttle, Luke escaped the main docking bay, just as that section began to blow apart completely. His wobbling craft, too, headed for the green sanctuary in the near distance.

And finally, as if being spit out of the very flames of the conflagration, the *Millennium Falcon* shot toward Endor, only moments before the Death Star flared into brilliant oblivion, like a fulminant supernova.

Han was binding Leia's arm-wound in a fern-dell when the Death Star blew. It captured everyone's attention, wherever they happened to be—Ewoks, stormtrooper prisoners, Rebel troops—this final, turbulent, flash of self-destruction, incandescent in the evening sky. The Rebels cheered.

Leia touched Han's cheek. He leaned over, and kissed her; then sat back, seeing her eyes focused on the starry sky.

"Hey," he jostled, "I'll bet Luke got off that thing before it blew."

She nodded. "He did. I can feel it." Her brother's living presence touched her, through the Force. She reached out to answer the touch, to reassure Luke she was all right. Everything was all right.

Han looked at her with deep love, special love. For she was a special woman. A princess not by title, but by heart. Her fortitude astounded him, yet she held herself so lightly. Once, he'd wanted whatever he wanted, for himself, because he wanted it. Now he wanted everything for her. *Her* everythings. And one thing he could see she wanted dearly, was Luke.

"You really care for him, don't you?"

She nodded, scanning the sky. He was alive, Luke was alive. And the other—the Dark One—was dead.

"Well, listen," Han went on, "I understand. When he gets back, I won't stand in your way..."

She squinted at him, suddenly aware they were

crossing wires, having different conversations. "What
are you talking about?" she said. Then she realized
what he was talking about. "Oh, no. No," she laughed,
"it's not like that at all—Luke is my *brother*."

Han was successively stunned, embarrassed, and
elated. This made *everything* fine, just fine.

He took her in his arms, embraced her, lowered her
back down into the ferns...and being extra careful of
her wounded arm, lay down there beside her, under
the waning glow of the burning Star.

Luke stood in a forest clearing before a great pile
of logs and branches. Lying, still and robed, atop the
mound, was the lifeless body of Darth Vader. Luke set
a torch to the kindling.

As the flames enveloped the corpse, smoke rose from
the vents in the mask, almost like a black spirit, finally
freed. Luke stared with a fierce sorrow at the conflagration. Silently, he said his last goodbye. He, alone,
had believed in the small speck of humanity remaining
in his father. That redemption rose, now, with these
flames, into the night.

Luke followed the blazing embers as they sailed to
the sky. They mixed, there, in his vision, with the fireworks the Rebel fighters were setting off in victory
celebration. And these, in turn, mingled with the bonfires that speckled the woods and the Ewoks village—
fires of elation, of comfort and triumph. He could hear
the drums beating, the music weaving in the firelight,
the cheers of brave reunion. Luke's cheer was mute as
he gazed into the fires of his own victory and loss.

A huge bonfire blazed in the center of the Ewok
village square for the celebration that night. Rebels
and Ewoks rejoiced in the warm firelight of the cool
evening—singing, dancing, and laughing, in the com-
munal language of liberation. Even Teebo and Artoo
had reconciled, and were doing a little jig together, as
others clapped in time to the music. Threepio, his regal
days in this village over, was content to sit near the

spinning little droid who was his best friend in the universe. He thanked the Maker that Captain Solo had been able to fix Artoo, not to mention Mistress Leia—for a man without protocol, Solo did have his moments. And he thanked the Maker this bloody war was over.

The prisoners had been sent on shuttles to what was left of the Imperial Fleet—the Rebel Star Cruisers were dealing with all that. Up there, somewhere. The Death Star had burned itself out.

Han, Leia, and Chewbacca stood off a short way from the revelers. They stayed close to each other, not talking; periodically glancing at the path that led into the village. Half waiting, half trying not to wait; unable to do anything else.

Until, at last, their patience was rewarded: Luke and Lando, exhausted but happy, stumbled down the path, out of the darkness, into the light. The friends rushed to greet them. They all embraced, cheered, jumped about, fell over, and finally just huddled, still wordless, content with the comfort of each other's touch.

In a while, the two droids sidled over as well, to stand beside their dearest comrades.

The fuzzy Ewoks continued in wild jubilation, far into the night, while this small company of gallant adventurers watched on from the sidelines.

For an evanescent moment, looking into the bonfire, Luke thought he saw faces dancing—Yoda, Ben; was it his father? He drew away from his companions, to try to see what the faces were saying; they were ephemeral, and spoke only to the shadows of the flames, and then disappeared altogether.

It gave Luke a momentary sadness but then Leia took his hand, and drew him back close to her and to the others, back into their circle of warmth, and camaraderie; and love.

The Empire was dead.

Long live the Alliance.

STAR TREK: THE WRATH OF KHAN

Vonda N. McIntyre

Having returned intact from both a five-year exploratory mission and an encounter with V'ger, the crew of the *Enterprise* have been given new assignments. Kirk, Spock and McCoy all based on Earth training cadets; Chekov — now first officer of the *Reliant* — has been sent on a top-secret mission. He must find a lifeless planet suitable for the final tests on the Genesis project — a project which will result in either unimaginable wealth or total devastation.

Unwittingly they land on a planet inhabited by the exiled and evil Khan and his cronies, who quickly trap them. And sensing that Chekov is in trouble, the *Enterprise* abandons a training voyage to go to the rescue.

Unaware that the Galaxy's ultimate weapon is in the hands of their enemy, Kirk and his crew fly heedless into a battle which will rock the universe, and mark the beginning of the Galaxy's greatest adventure ever!

Fiction/Film Tie-In
0 7088 2220 7

THE DARK CRYSTAL

A. C. H. Smith

Out of time and place, the world of *The Dark Crystal* is both beautiful and strange, secret and frightening: a world of creatures beyond experience. And dominating all is the mystery and power of *The Dark Crystal*.

In the Castle Of The Dark Crystal, the cruel Skeksis learn with fear of an ancient prophecy: a survivor of a survivor of the Gelfings will restore *The Dark Crystal* and destroy their evil power. The story of Jen the Gelfing and his quest now joins the ranks of epic fantasy fiction in this powerful novel of adventure and imagination.

The Dark Crystal is based on the movie produced by Jim Henson and Gary Kurtz, directed by Jim Henson and Frank Oz, screenplay by David Odell, and conceptual design by Brian Froud.

Fiction/Film Tie-In
0 7088 2231 2

ALIEN

Alan Dean Foster

With a crew of seven and a cargo of two billion tons of fossil fuels, the deep space tug crawled across the outer reaches of the galaxy.

Whilst the computer guided the ship, the humans slept – until the Nostromo's scanners picked up a garbled distress call from a remote and long dead planet. And all the technology of the future could not shield them from the nightmare of today.

For on the planet, something stirred . . . something alien.

Once aboard their vast and labyrinthine craft it killed to live – and lived to kill . . .

Fiction/Film Tie-In
0 7088 1678 9

All Futura Books are available at your bookshop or newsagent, or can be ordered from the following address:
Futura Books, Cash Sales Department,
P.O. Box 11, Falmouth, Cornwall.

Please send cheque or postal order (no currency), and allow 45p for postage and packing for the first book plus 20p for the second book and 14p for each additional book ordered up to a maximum charge of £1.63 in U.K.

Customers in Eire and B.F.P.O. please allow 45p for the first book, 20p for the second book plus 14p per copy for the next 7 books, thereafter 8p per book.

Overseas customers please allow 75p for postage and packing for the first book and .21p per copy for each additional book.

Join the Official Star Wars™ Fan Club

Members of the Official Star Wars Fan Club receive a special Jedi membership kit containing:

> Full colour Jedi poster
> 6 Full colour Jedi Photographs
> Full colour Jedi decal
> Multi-coloured Jedi patch
> Jedi membership card
> 4 Issues of Bantha Tracks, the Club's official newsletter

The membership fee is £4.25. Crossed cheques or postal orders made payable to Official Star Wars Fan Club should be sent to:

> Star Wars Fan Club
> P O Box 284
> Maldon
> Essex CM9 6EY

Do not send cash. Please allow 4 to 6 weeks for delivery.